VICTRIX

Also in this trilogy so far...

Victoria

VICTRIX

FRANCES HENDRY

Hodder
Children's
Books

A division of Hodder Headline Limited

From the author

In about 64CE every Roman city had an arena where violent, deadly fights and hunts were put on for the brutal pleasure of the spectators. Blood and death were never far away, whether in the ring, on the streets, or among the greedy, decadent magistrates and officials of the Empire. People had to be tough, strong, brave – and lucky – just to stay alive. Thousands didn't.

As in the first book of the set, 'Victoria', I've tried to reflect this world for people of today without glamorising it, or skirting the realities, or wallowing in gore. But to my character, Victoria, it was reality.

I have to confess that in this book I have adapted history, just a little. A murder that I place before the Fire of Rome probably happened after it; and I have used the most scandal-mongering, malevolent historians of the time as a source for my family history of Nero. Apart from that, the history and atmosphere of Pompeii and Rome are as accurate as I can make them. Emperor Nero did indeed, among other things, murder his mother, give a huge estate to a gladiator named Spiculus, worship a small carved ivory idol that he kept among his pillows, and get a senator to ride an elephant down a tightrope.

Don't look for the palaestra of Glaevius in Pompeii; it's in the bit that has not been excavated yet. The houses of Julia Felix and Popidius Ampliatus, however, are there. Nero's palace at Baiae has been destroyed and built over, but it did have hot baths from the local volcanic springs. Among the statues of Amazons in the Museo Archaeologico in Naples, Victoria is the second from the right, though it's not a very good likeness.

I hope you enjoy the book.

Frances Mary Hendry

I

'You wish to become a gladiatrix? Hmm. Why?'

Glaevius was no-one you would pick out of a crowd, until you noticed the shrewd, rock-hard eyes, the immobile face, the scars. A handspan shorter than Victoria, as most Romans were, he wore a formal white tunic of good wool, and a gold stud in one ear. He studied her closely, as she studied him.

Hiding her nervousness, Victoria perched on the edge of a cushioned stool. The room was painted rich saffron, with an energetic fresco of gladiators – what else, here? – facing a wide window that gave a fine view of towering Mount Vesuvius.

'Your accent says you are from Britain? We get good fighters from there.'

Victoria told a very edited and mostly-true version of her story. She was the daughter of a merchant of Londinium and an Iceni woman, always in trouble for her temper. She had run away to her mother's family, had started training to become a warrior with them, but when the Iceni queen, Boudicca, rose in rebellion against Rome she had to leave. She did not mention her experiences during the war, nor the terrible geas – the sacred task laid on her by Boudicca.

'My father would not take me back. So, I decided to become a gladiatrix. I can fight with a sword, and throw a spear, and drive a chariot. I walked to Massilia, to a lanista I had been told about, called Bombio. But he said he'd never trained a Mars-cursed woman, and by Mars's nuts he was too Mars-blessed old to start now.'

Glaevius chuckled abruptly. 'I know old Bombio, I can hear him saying it!'

'He told me to come to you, here in Pompeii. He said you were the best lanista in the world, your school here is modern, the best, better than the traditional ones in Capua, and you show the finest gladiators. And gladiatrixes. So I came here.'

'Good of the old man to say so. But correct. I produce better fighters than any other lanista, no clumsy sword-fodder. So, they are expensive to hire, but popular. They fight maybe once in two months, not every tenth day till they're killed as happens with some. They are well trained, they fight skilfully, they live longer than those from any other school, they more often win freedom, fame and fortune. Therefore I have a large school, and many volunteers, though I pay no enlistment bounty. My female fighters are renowned, they are able to face men as well as fighting other gladiatrixes and dwarfs in comedy combats. Shocking, but the crowd loves it.' He eyed her thoughtfully. 'But I do not take on just anyone. What if I refuse you?'

After coming all this way! She made herself shrug coolly. 'I'll find another lanista who will accept me. And make him as famous as you are.'

At that he barked a laugh. 'I suppose a good conceit of yourself is part of being a Gaul.'

'A Briton.'

His eyes narrowed slightly. 'You contradict me? If I want to display you as a black Ethiop, or a slit-eyed yellow woman from the east, you will paint up without argument!' He was not too displeased, though, at her show of spirit. 'So. You have some training, and no anxious mother or lover to encourage you to drop out halfway through your training.'

'No. I'll stay.' Victoria held herself still and resolute as he studied her again.

'Hmm.' At length he nodded. 'Very well. I shall take you, if you pass my tests. You will bind yourself legally to me for five years or fifty fights. The normal is three years, or thirty fights. I ask more, for I offer more. I shall feed, train and arm you, look after your health, arrange fair fights for you. I shall throw you out with a small payment, if you are crippled or if you fall ill. If you decide to leave, you buy yourself out at your worth – my estimate – in the slave market. As a volunteer, I shall not sell you without your consent, but if you run, you are a fugitive slave and I shall crucify you. Three-quarters of any prize money you win is mine; all gifts are yours. If you last, we can discuss a new contract. You risk losing your life; I risk losing money on your training and care. We could both do well out of it. Well?'

'Yes.' To impress this man she kept her voice firm, decisive, showing neither her apprehension nor her delight. 'What tests?'

He snorted with cold mirth again. 'Not a chatterbox, are you? Good.' His cold black eyes studied her. Finally he nodded. 'Come along and see if you can convince my chief trainer, Pulcher, and then my physician, that you are worth training. I have no chariot handy, but a sword we can always supply.'

Victoria followed the lanista down the narrow stair to the tunnel that led to the outside gate. A guard slid back four solid bolts in the gate at the inner end of the tunnel and heaved it open.

The light, heat and din from the palaestra, the exercise yard, hit Victoria like a wall.

The space was nearly a hundred paces long by eighty wide. Guards on a head-high walkway all round the walls stiffened to alertness as the boss appeared. Below them, well over a hundred men were training, in loincloths, kilts, tunics or bare skin. Three-quarters wore a metal collar, slaves, she supposed, while the others would be volunteers like herself.

A dozen were swinging heavy wooden clubs. Others were skipping, or boxing with padded mittens, wrestling, or even, to her amazement, walking on their hands. How could that help you fight? At one side, some were thrusting tridents at a row of straw dummies jerking wildly on ropes.

Twenty heavy wooden posts the height of a man, set about three paces apart in a hollow square in the middle of the yard, were being battered with wooden swords, fast and hard, on the yell of the command, 'Four two four eight three four one – six times and put a bit of beef in it, you soft dollies! Go!' A pattern of blows, she realised.

In the central space three pairs were fighting under the eyes of a trainer, in a clatter of wooden swords and shields. The trainer shouted at them to stop, talked, demonstrated a blow, waved them on.

Awed, Victoria gazed at a post that whirled long spars round and back, one beam at knee-height, another level with her shoulders. Three men were leaping and ducking the spars. How – Oh, it was turned by men pulling a rope wound round it—

'Out the way, girl!' She skipped aside from some men trotting past carrying heavy rocks.

A trainer struck one with a whippy rod. 'You dodge her, stumble-bum!' They circled the yard to a free-standing flight of uneven steps on the far side, ran up to the top, down the other side, back up and down again, then over once more to start round again.

She jumped again at a deep voice behind her. 'Sir?'

The speaker was as tall as Victoria, dark curls glossy in the

5

sunlight. His shockingly short leopard-skin tunic left long legs, a sleekly muscled, bronzed torso and one broad shoulder gleaming in the morning sun. She almost smirked. Didn't he think he was something! She despised handsome, conceited men . . .

Then her breath caught as she saw his face. Something had sliced twice, right across his face. One hideous scar ran from his left temple across his eyebrow, twisting it askew; then across the bridge of his nose and down his right cheek. The other ran from his left cheekbone across his mouth, distorting his lips into a permanent bitter half-smile. Imprisoned in this wrecked cage, intelligent dark-brown eyes gleamed, alert for her reaction.

'Ah, Pulcher. A volunteer. Victoria,' Glaevius introduced her. 'Try her out.'

Pulcher meant beautiful. Who named him that, in jeering ridicule or irony? Older than herself, but not yet thirty. What a tragedy for him! But he defied his fate, wearing that extravagantly sexy tunic that would make an actor blush, ironically drawing attention to himself. Had she shown shock? She hoped not. It would hurt so badly . . .

Pulcher was studying her. 'You want to be a gladiatrix?'

She straightened self-consciously, dragging her gaze to meet his eyes. 'Yes, sir.'

'Hmm.' He walked round her, considering her. 'Strip.'

'Strip? Here – in front of all these . . . ?'

'If you want to join them, you join them. Worse will happen to you than embarrassment, girl. If you can't take it, the gate is behind you, leave while you can.'

Behind her the clacking thuds and shouting were fading. Everyone was stopping to stare. Pulcher gazed round sardonically. 'Rest time already?' The noise rose again.

Victoria's temper started to simmer, but she fought it down. This man would be in charge of her training. True, she had to do what the rest did – and he wasn't making her a show just for fun.

This morning she had carefully wrapped up nose to toes like a decent Roman girl, only her face peering from the shapeless cocoon of dark blue wool. She loosened her wrap round her shoulders, and drew a deep, nervous breath. Right. She had planned and practised this; now to see if it worked.

She spun, whirling the cloth flying above her like a banner. Under it she wore her brightest Iceni clothes: red checked shirt, yellow-and-black striped trousers, blue leather jerkin and sandals. Her sword Needle was slung in front of her waist, to hang unnoticed between her knees if she sat down. She swept it high, shrieking a war-cry that stilled the yard to sudden silence. Glaevius and Pulcher both leapt away in swift reaction as, in one second, she turned from a big, lumpy, respectable girl into a warrior of the Iceni ready for battle, the shocking swirl of tattoos on her scalp blazing across the exercise yard.

Fine so far. What next? Keep going? Keep going!

Victoria stuck her sword point into a trestle and set her hands on her belt buckle, grinning defiantly. 'You want me to go right down?'

From all round arose a chorus of whistles, laughter and clapping. Even Glaevius's lips twitched.

Pulcher's didn't. 'What do you think this is, a pantomime?' He glanced round; training recommenced at once.

'I wondered why you were sweltering like that.' Glaevius eyed her head with interest. 'Hmm. You realise that half the show is showmanship. Good.'

Pulcher nodded towards the sword. 'Can you use that?'

She grinned tightly. 'How hard can it be? You stick the pointy end in.'

He didn't laugh. He sighed. 'Another smart-arse.'

She glared. 'I've killed my man.' More than one, in fact, but she didn't want to talk about it.

Neither did he. He didn't look impressed as she had hoped; he sneered. 'That means you've a load of bad habits that we'll have to train out of you. Like that sword. We don't use steel here. Not for training. Nor keep it in the barracks, not with slaves about.'

She bristled. 'I don't give Needle up for anyone!'

'It has a name? A real barbarian trick! Then leave,' he challenged her, raising an eyebrow towards Glaevius, who nodded.

Losing Needle would be like losing an arm. But if it was the only way . . . 'All right.'

Glaevius grunted satisfaction. 'Yes, you are determined. I shall keep it safe for you. You might even use it in the ring.'

As Victoria's face cleared, Pulcher jerked his head disdainfully at her. 'Let's see if you fight as well as you act.'

Victoria laid her scabbard and wrap on the trestle beside Needle. The noise was dying again – the men were stopping training, to spectate. This time Pulcher allowed it. She glanced round at the grins, the expectant eyes. They wanted a show? She'd show them!

In the open square in the middle the fighters stood aside. One offered her his wooden sword and small shield.

'Ready?' Suddenly Pulcher's wooden sword smacked her left arm. She cursed indignantly, and then was being chased all over the palaestra. Pulcher was fast, stabbing, weaving, driving her among the posts. The other men leapt clear, cheering and jeering. Curse him, curse this curved sword, it was oddly balanced, the shield was too small, he was making her look like a fool! She ducked round a post from one side to the other, left, right, left, suddenly doubled back, parried a blow harder than he had expected, and thrust in return. He jumped back, and for a minute they exchanged blows. She was getting used to the sword – he dropped back, she advanced gleefully, got him on the run—

Her sword suddenly jolted out of her grasp, flying away to clatter against the wall on the far side of the yard. She cursed again as Pulcher's blade whacked her bottom, and the crowd jeered. But then he nodded, lips twisted derisively. 'I suppose my old granny would do worse.'

Not panting, he led her back towards Glaevius. 'Fairly fit, not bad balance. Her wrist's strong, her eye's straight, quick reactions, and she's not shy of being hit. She's been taught a bit, by a cavalryman, and she's used to fighting longer weapons – spears maybe, or long Gaulish swords. Her knees are stiff. No idea about using a shield, and the left hand is very weak. But she learns fast.' He shrugged. 'Worth a try, if Manny can fix the hand and knees.'

'How could you tell all that?' she demanded. 'About the cavalryman?'

Glaevius smiled slightly. 'He has fought in the arena for thirteen years, girl. There is little he cannot tell about an opponent after one minute. If he says you are worth training—'

'You'll take me on?' Her grin was ecstatic. She turned it on Pulcher. 'Oh, thank you!'

He shrugged a dismissive shoulder. 'Thank me again next year – if you're still alive.' Her smile faded as his sourness, and those horrible scars which made her clench her teeth to hide disgust, threw a bucket of grit in the high smooth glide of her joy.

Glaevius nodded. 'Take her over to see Manny, and if he passes her, bring her to the shrine.'

Pulcher gestured to a row of low doors along the far wall. 'Come along, then. It's the end door. And here's the reason that brought you to our gate.'

On the high steps, perched like spectators at the games, sat a dozen of the people Victoria had come to join: the gladiatrixes.

'Girls, this is Victoria.'

They studied her, as she studied them, with intense interest. They were of assorted sizes and ages. Victoria thought she was the youngest; the oldest was perhaps thirty. Four were mid-brown, one with oddly slanted eyes in a broad face. Two were really dark-skinned; one almost black, tall, thin and languid with a fuzz of hair round her head, the other a giantess, a rich deep brown, heavy-muscled, with longer black locks. One big-boned, hulking woman looked like a Gaul, her pale skin freckled like gravel, her hair light reddish fawn. One was very blonde. The rest had dark brown or black hair, plaited or tied tight back. They wore bright, worn tunics, or kilts and leather bodices. Five wore slave collars. All bore scars, gravel grazes, and deep bruises. Rather to Victoria's surprise, only one was ugly – atrociously scarred all over – but all looked hard, fit, tough enough to chew hobnailed boots; fighting women.

Killing women.

Would she have to kill them? Would one of them kill her?

At length one of the older women slid down off the steps, and strolled round Victoria, inspecting her. She was the smallest, only up to Victoria's shoulder; dark and almost dainty in a pink tunic, but wiry and strong. Her hands bore swordsman's calluses. Victoria started at a touch on her scalp. 'Tattoos, over scars,' the woman commented. 'he rest pursed their lips thoughtfully. 'How you get that, girl?'

'A burning house fell on me.'

Pulcher's eyebrows rose in fresh interest. The thin black woman laughed, her mouth wide and red, her teeth startling white. Another woman spat in contempt. Behind Victoria, the slim woman chuckled. 'Burn hair away? So make display. Not bad!' She came round to face Victoria, and touched her chest. 'Divina. I lead women. You do what I say or I hit you stupid head.'

'You can try, Mistress Divina.' Victoria bowed respectfully.

Barking a laugh, Divina waved a hand to the rest. 'Africa, Hippolyta, Thraex, Scilla, Ferocia . . .' Heads nodded. Victoria nodded and smiled, though she could only pick out the freckled Gaul, Gallia, Thraex, the scarred one, Ferocia, the unfriendly one – who sneered, 'You'll be sorry!' – and thin black Africa, the only one who smiled.

Pulcher interrupted. 'You'll learn them all soon. Right, Divina, get on. Group six will be off the posts soon, and then it's your turn. Only the best win glory!'

12

The women dropped lithely off the steps and gathered in a loose circle, picking up three head-sized stones. They began to toss the stones across the circle, fast. Whenever a stone was dropped they all jeered, 'Greasy-fingers!' Then Divina called, 'Left!' They began to skip sideways as they threw the stones, moving faster and faster. The drops became more frequent until they got the rhythm; but before they could settle into it, Divina called, 'Right!' and the circle reversed direction.

Victoria stood entranced as they danced round, the stones flying. 'It strengthens arms and grip, balance, reactions,' Pulcher explained.

'I could never – Yes! Yes, I'll keep up! I'll do it!'

His lips quirked sideways. 'If Manny says you're fit enough.'

'Who's Manny?'

'Immanuel ben Judah. Our physician. We have our own, not like the smaller schools who call one in at need – often him. In here. A volunteer, Manny. Check her over, will you?'

The physician was an elderly slave, plump and dark, his eyebrows impressively flaring, his nose impressively hooked. He examined Victoria's eyes, teeth, bones and muscles, probed every scar till she gritted her teeth not to wince. She had to bend and stretch, skip, breathe deeply, lift weights, all the time aware of Pulcher's eyes on her. Worse things than embarrassment . . . At least he didn't comment bawdily as some would have, he just watched coldly. Manny spent a lot of time on her left hand and her knees. 'Grip my wrist with all

13

your force . . . Now open the hand as far as it will go. Hmm. What happened? A fire? Hmm.'

At last, he nodded to her to dress again. 'The left hand and knees are damaged, as you know, sir,' he reported. 'However, they can be strengthened.'

'Enough?' Pulcher sounded doubtful.

'Certainly, sir. Opening the hand, rather than gripping, will be the problem. I fear that it and her knees may well bother her in age, should Yahweh allow her to live so long, but for the arena, for the time being—'

'She'll do?'

Manny shrugged. 'In my estimation, yes.'

Victoria couldn't help it; in relief and delight she gave a war-shriek, startling the men. She just grinned at Manny's stare and Pulcher's scornful smile. She was in!

Back at the gate, Pulcher knocked. A small hatch opened at head height for the guard to check who was there, before the bolts were drawn and the door opened. No risk of the slaves breaking out.

In the entrance tunnel, in a wide, shallow niche painted dark red, stood a bowl of powdered incense and a little lamp in front of a dozen statuettes and pictures, and a painted plaster bust of the Emperor.

Glaevius appeared at the doorway to the stairs, a paper in his hand. At Pulcher's nod, he turned to Victoria. 'By which gods will you swear obedience and loyalty? Most of the women

14

pray to Diana the huntress, or Hercules like the men. Or we have Fortuna, Mars, Horus, Mithras for ex-soldiers, Mercury the guide of the dead, or here is your own namesake, the goddess Victoria—'

'Victoria. I'll swear by her, but as Bouda, that's what we call her.'

'Ah? Yes, your ring name could be Boudicca, like the savage queen—'

'No!' His eyes widened slightly at the force of her protest, and she stopped herself. 'I'm sorry, sir. But no. Not that. I'll never . . . I thought I'd call myself Victrix, it's near my own name.'

'Victrix.' He tasted the name. 'Victrix. The conqueror. Yes. Good. So, Victrix. In return for my best efforts to train you as a gladiatrix, do you give your oath before Bouda, goddess of victory, and before Eternal Rome and the Emperor Nero, and before all gods, to take me as your legal master for five years; to serve faithfully and willingly? Do you swear to submit to burning iron, fetters, whip or steel, at my order?'

This was the dreadful gladiator's oath, putting herself fully into the power of the lanista. Branding . . . chains . . . flogging . . . death.

Victoria swallowed, in a dry throat. But only a coward turned back from a known and chosen path. She stiffened her neck, sprinkled a pinch of the sweet-scented incense onto the flame of the lamp with a steady hand, and drew a deep breath.

15

It was the last she would draw in freedom for five years. 'I call Bouda and Rome, Nero and all gods and spirits to witness. I swear it.'

II

Victoria shared a small, windowless dormitory with five other volunteers. As the newest trainees she and Atalanta had the rope beds farthest from the door, and so the stuffiest. They had storage space below, and a couple of hanging pegs above, for as volunteers they were allowed to keep their own clothes, and the heavy door was not locked at night. She was glad not to be locked in next door with vicious Ferocia and the bought slaves.

Divina, on her third contract, had won her freedom. She had her own room and could go out as she pleased after training. She looked fragile and feminine, but struck with the speed and accuracy of a snake. She was rich already with prize money, expensive to hire, and very popular outside the arena too, in spite of – or because of – her broken Latin. 'Men like. Feel big, clever. So why bother learn speak good, eh?' She added a dirty joke, surprising in her soft, tinkly voice, but advised Victoria, 'For you, no men, you too – too warm. Africa, me, yes, but you no stay cold-heart, you tangle, lose sharp, lose life!'

Victoria thoroughly agreed. She remembered her father beating her and her mother. No; definitely no men. In any case, she worked too hard to have time or energy to spare.

Socially a gladiator was the lowest of the low. She herself, when she started playing at sword-fighting in Londinium – so long ago, it seemed! – she had despised them as scum, looked down on even by beggars and slaves. Now, though, she learned to respect them.

Most were slaves from all over the world, sullen or violent troublemakers brought in by infuriated owners or bought cheap in the slave markets, or prisoners of war, picked for their aggressiveness. Now they had to fight for Glaevius, willingly or to avoid whipping, or be killed to encourage the rest. They might live, and win to fame and even freedom, but the chances were heavy against it. They would probably die early, as novices. Victoria often heard sobbing and sometimes screaming in the night, calling on gods or lost families, but next day they hid their pain, their fear, shame and despair, and got on with the job.

She did the same herself; in all the world, no-one was left who knew where she was, or cared. She too was alone, friendless, self-reliant. She embraced their fierce pride in themselves, in their perilous, deadly skills. Yes, many were brutal, bitter, vicious, foul-mouthed, but not all. She came to appreciate their defiant valour, their bleak and bawdy humour, their endurance of a life whose harshness would destroy most of the civilians outside who sneered at them – and admired them.

Life was not all bad. Glaevius fed his people well. The food was plain but plentiful, and she didn't have to hunt or cook it or clear up. As much lentil porridge and bread as she wanted mid-morning, and at dinner, just before sunset, the stews held a fair amount of fish or sausage, with cabbage, turnip and parsnip, peas, lupins and beans, celery and lettuce salads, and occasionally fruit. You ate everything the cook slaves dolloped into your wooden bowl; fads and fancies were not allowed, but if there was any left you could ask for more. Victoria learned to like garlic and the salty fish sauce that Romans sprinkled over everything, and loved the tough, basil-flavoured pizza breads.

After four days, she collapsed on her straw mattress. 'Thank the gods! They drive us like slaves!' she puffed to Africa, lounging on the bed by the door.

The tall woman glanced sideways at her, grinning. 'Slaves? What else d'you think you are, dummy, for five years?'

It was a sobering thought.

Her room-mates were coming in after her, from washing and massage. Tigris was easing a shoulder. 'By Hercules, that new Egyptian masseur enjoys his work! Fingers like flamin' grapplin' irons! But he's doin' me arm good.'

Victoria had two painful massage sessions every day, but pain was just part of the job. Complaining about cuts and grazes from falling on the gravel, bruises and aching muscles, even broken toes and fingers and lost teeth – for wooden swords were as hard as iron ones – gained mockery, not sympathy. Sore stomachs and headaches were beneath mentioning. 'Maybe it's the ointment that's helping,' she suggested.

Tigris shrugged. 'Maybe. Don't matter, as long as somethin' works. Arnica stinks, eh? Ferocia were gripin' at you about the smell when you was wrestlin', weren't she? Worser'n ten weasels wi' toothache, her, same wi' everybody, never pay her no heed.'

'I wish Glaevius would heat the pool water like the baths in town,' Hippolyta commented, combing out her long blonde hair.

Atalanta agreed enthusiastically. She had joined only a month before Victoria. 'I'd give my right arm – well, you know what I mean – for hot baths in here.'

'Hark at Empress Poppaea!' Thraex snorted. Blushing, Atalanta subsided.

'Oh, it's wonderful in this heat!' Victoria protested. And though they jeered, she insisted, 'In Britain we don't have baths, just rivers or the sea, cold enough to freeze your – well, really cold! This is only pleasantly cool, in comparison.' She grinned at their snorts of disbelief. 'No, honest! It feels good, getting rid of the grit and sweat. And private, with the men kept out while we're in.'

Stretching lazily, Africa laughed – the soft, furry chuckle that men found so attractive. 'Divina's right, girl, you're a real shy violet! But yes, we're lucky. The other schools all use the town palaestra pool, men an' women together, the girls there get a lot of hassle. Not that they don't enjoy it, most of 'em.'

'I wish Glaevius would lay in a better water supply. It smells sometimes.' Tigris wrinkled her nose. 'Specially if the men go in first.'

'Men are stinking pigs.' Thraex was an ex-slave, her skin ridged all over from floggings and burnings. Victoria had learned fast that you mustn't ask about anyone's former life, but you could easily see why Thraex hated men.

As Africa, who didn't, started to sit up to argue, Hippolyta changed the subject to keep the peace. 'How's your leg, Thraex?'

The stocky girl scratched an inflamed wound. 'Mending. Manny's the only cursed man I know that's any use. But I got the cursed scorpion in the end. He'll not scar anybody else!'

This gave Victoria the lead she had been hoping for. 'Talking about scars—'

'We don't know,' Tigris interrupted her, and laughed at Victoria's surprise. 'Pulcher, right? He joined before Divina or any of us, wi' that face already, ain't a ring wound. Called hisself Pulcher. Valerius was here then, the trident trainer – ye know they're all ex-gladiators? Aye, well, he says his second day, just, Pulcher killed a man as jeered at him, a second-year man, an' him a untrained lad wi' just a wooden sword, but that fast an' ragin' unexpected nobody could stop him in time.'

'More power to his arm!' Thraex cheered.

'Lucky, too,' Tigris nodded. 'Glaevius could've crucified him, but he just whopped him, an' then said if anybody mocked his face again he'd punish 'em on top o' whatever Pulcher done to 'em. Wouldn't waste a fighter like that, right? Pulcher's quality-born, a flamin' patrician, but nobody don't know his family or what happened. Well, Glaevius, I s'pose, but he's close as a clam.'

'Yes. If you find out, tell us!' Africa rolled into her blanket. 'Now shut up, you chattering starlings, I want to sleep.' She was the boss of the room; they settled down quietly.

Killed a man for laughing at him? What pride – and despair! Victoria's cousin Cram back home in Britain was like that, embittered by fate's cruelty. She sympathised.

Every morning everybody ran round the yard a hundred times, half weaving each way to practise dodging. They raced backwards and forwards over the irregular steps, driven on faster and faster by shouts and blows from the trainers. Then they did it again – backwards. 'Think you'll always be attacking, dumbo?' When Victoria could dodge automatically, she got heavy and awkward objects to carry while she ran: a big stone, a full-sized knee-to-shoulder army shield, a bulky bundle of canvas, a tree-trunk, a bowl full of water – or a mouthful, which was worse – or a person, piggy-back or over a shoulder.

22

Every few days they went out for a long training run, as legionary soldiers did; ten or fifteen miles, bunched within a ring of rope surrounded by guards, the slaves in the centre, carrying heavier packs every time, urged on to speed by the trainers' whippy rods. In time Victoria's knees stopped screaming at her.

Inside the school, on the palaestra, the odd things they did astonished her at first. In one corner they had to stand in turn inside a small circle while three of the others threw stones at them. Victoria learned fast how to fend off most stones with her small square shield, and twist to avoid the others. They juggled with these egg-sized stones, and leapt round tossing big ones. They danced, wrestled and did acrobatics, rolls, somersaults and flips, all in heavy boiled-leather practice armour; 'Go down, and you get up flaming fast or die!'

On her second day Pulcher had called her into the centre. 'Let's find out what style suits you. Forget what you think you know. You're starting from the beginning.'

'No, I'm not!'

He had welted her ribs for impertinence, and quickly proved her wrong, his rod alone against her sword and shield.

Fencing with Dio in Londinium, training to be an Iceni warrior, even fighting in a battle was all like a child's hobby, compared to this. This was professional.

Under Pulcher's keen eye and sardonic tongue, she was tested with four different swords and three kinds of shield. A

23

small shield was like a boxing glove with a blunt spike and sharp edges; it could parry or turn a thrust, and then dart forward to bang or cut an enemy's face and arms. A heavy army shield was not just protection from shoulder to knee; if your opponent's weapon stuck in the leather-covered wood you could hope to twist it aside, maybe right out of his grip, or hold it aside to let you strike round it, or maybe just drop your shield to weigh down the wedged blade and wade in, swinging with both hands for a quick kill.

She learned how to use her armoured arm to parry a blow, and where to strike to kill fast, or to cripple, to make your opponent flinch, or to draw lots of blood to weaken her – or him. Women usually fought women, or dwarfs in comedy fights, but Glaevius's girls were changing that.

So, she also learned how to kill and be killed with mercy and grace.

'If you can't go on, wounded or disarmed, you kneel, hang on to your opponent's leg for support if you need to, and raise a hand. If the crowd like you, want you to live and fight for them again, they'll wave their hands upwards. Then the winner parades round the arena, being cheered, while the arena slaves help you – or if necessary carry you – off to the surgeons. But if the crowd dislike you they'll stab down with their thumbs. Then the winner will finish you off quickly with a stab under the helmet.' Pulcher tapped the back of his neck.

'So if I win, I may have to kill a helpless man?' She was alarmed. 'I can't!'

'Dumbo! What did you think you'd joined, a working men's social club? A trip to the seaside? Just make it quick and clean. We're fighters, not torturers. And if the crowd calls for death and you refuse, the games editor will kill your opponent anyway, and you'll be executed too,' he warned her briskly.

Divina was shocked. 'Refuse? You not dare! I kill you myself!'

And Africa. 'You'd disgrace Glaevius, and all of us!'

'The games started as funeral rites, a sacrifice to the spirit of the dead, and to the gods. Nowadays, the games also get the spectators used to blood and death. Apart from the excitement, we teach them that if even criminals or slaves can fight and die bravely, freemen can and must do more.' For once Pulcher was not sneering. 'We do the fighting and bleeding, killing and dying for the crowd's fun – and education. We know it's hard. That's why we discourage friendships.'

Victoria looked at him, and at the women round her, in dawning dismay. He nodded. 'Glaevius tries to get the games editors to arrange combats against strangers from other schools, but you'll often have to fight someone you know. Even then, it's not so hard to kill in the speed and excitement of the contest, when you may live or die at the slip of a foot, the twist of a hilt in your fist. Deliberately finishing a comrade, though – that is painful. But it must be done.'

Divina agreed. 'That why full-head helmet. Easier fight an' kill friend if no face, just mask. Easiest if not friend.'

Victoria shivered. That was why some of them wouldn't talk to her.

At the trestle tables for supper that evening, Victoria settled down beside the head woman with her bowl of mutton stew and a couple of rounds of bread. 'Divina, can I ask you something? If it's harder to kill someone whose face is seen, surely a retiarius, with no helmet, is safer?' A retiarius fought with net and trident like a fisherman, left arm armoured and head protected by a high-flaring shoulder-guard. She had tried it that afternoon. However, after watching her tangle her trident, net and feet till she fell over in a helpless huddle, Pulcher had sniffed in disgust and tossed her her wooden sword again.

Divina, picking disdainfully at her stew, laughed. 'You tied in net – flaming funny!' She considered Victoria thoughtfully. 'Not retiarius, you. Vain, show off pretty faces. Popular, but not last long, unless real quick-feet. You not. Not clumsy, but not –' She pattered her hands rapidly on the table to indicate fast footwork, and then shook her head. 'Atalanta do, but slow-feet. First fight, she die, I think.' The thought did not trouble her; you had to be hard in the palaestra, and though she looked slender and delicate her mind was as tough as her muscles. 'Africa do three, four year now.'

'I can see why she's lasted. That lazy grace tricks people into thinking she's slow.'

'An' make many fans, crowd two times vote to live when she beat.'

In the evenings Victoria took off the scarf she wore to protect her scarred scalp from the blazing Italian sun. Now Divina eyed the swirls of colour. 'You got good trick, when you win, take off helmet. Crowd go crazy for you!' She touched the gold bells that always dangled at her ears. 'I do with these. Big earrings on helmet, not feathers – even half-blind grandads know me.'

'The helmet's so hot and stuffy, though – it's stifling!'

'Better have than not have. Like head. Maybe you wear open-face one. You like, eh? Ask Pulcher, Glaevius. But I think they say no.' She considered. 'Secutor, provocator, myrmillo, even Samnite, they heavy – big shield, much armour, arms, legs. Too flaming much. Gallia, Alexandria can carry; but you tall, not solid. Most women want move quick, fight Thracian, like me.' She carried the small square shield and the curved sword that had bothered Victoria during her trial; her right arm was armoured and greaves protected her knees and shins. 'Or hoplomachus, little round shield an' spear, like Tigris, can't use sword, but spear, oh yes, yes, flaming yes! But you like sword? So. Thracian.'

★ ★ ★

Now Victoria was set to spar with other girls, and men, while the trainers called advice, criticism, encouragement, and used a cane freely to spur her on. Often she had a bout with one of the trainers, too, and found, rather to her dismay, that she worked best and most often with Pulcher.

'The pointy end, remember, dozy? That's not a rolling-pin, don't try to break my skull with it, you're not my wife, thank the gods! Shield forward, nobody's attacking your flabby backside! Don't thrust so far, if I dodge – see? You can't get back fast enough. You're dead – and good riddance to a lumbering oaf!' His tongue was fiercely scathing, often worse than a cane.

Even when he was not teaching her directly, she was always conscious of him hovering, watching her, making her so nervous she grew clumsy. She felt like murdering him.

One day when she was running round the yard carrying Ferocia, she stumbled and dropped her passenger. As Ferocia bounced up, she gave Victoria a bang on the ear. 'Stupid clumsy flat-footed painty-head three-legged donkey!'

Victoria's hot temper flared. 'Poison-tongued toad!' She hit back, was knocked flying, and kicked Ferocia's knees to bring her down too.

While they tussled cursing across the gravel, Pulcher's voice snapped above them, 'Up, both of you!' Ferocia rolled away. When Victoria lunged after her, the trainer's cane lashed across her shoulder, and when she leapt up and turned on him, hands raised, he slashed her face.

Her temper exploded. She dived at him but somehow found herself wrenched round and slung across to where Divina and Alexandria jumped to hold her. 'Let me go! I'll gut them—' She struggled, screeched threats.

'Quiet, fool girl!' Divina hissed.

Glaevius was there instantly. 'Stand, girl. Still! Pulcher, what happened?'

Pulcher shrugged. 'The girls were squabbling. When I told them to stop, Victrix was too excited, she carried on. I hit her, she went for me.'

'Hmm.' Glaevius's eyes were colder even than normal. 'Did she hit you?' Pulcher snorted contempt. 'Very well.' Glaevius glared at where Victoria stood panting and beginning to realise that she was in really serious trouble. 'For attacking a trainer, you could be crucified.' She bared her teeth at him, still too angry to be afraid. 'However, as you did not reach him – a dozen lashes.' Victoria felt a moment's contempt – a dozen was nothing. Well – not much.

The whole school was paraded to watch. Divina and Africa stripped off Victoria's top and tied her wrists round one of the posts. 'Fool!' Divina muttered. 'Ferocia always make trouble! Keep temper!'

Glaevius jerked his head for Divina to step away to her place in front of the women. Victoria stood there, shaking with embarrassment and fury. How stupid she had been! But no matter how hard the guard struck, she'd not cry out! She was the cousin of a king!

Then a sudden agony burned across her back, drove her into the post, jolted her, locked all her muscles, stopped her breathing. She nearly screamed, despite her determination. Again, and again, and again . . . This was as bad as the fire when she had lost her hair. She had fought through that, she'd fight through this! But it got no easier. She clenched her teeth and forced herself to breathe.

After the last blow she was freed, to stand rigid, her face stiff, trying to stop herself trembling. Glaevius nodded. 'Learn control. That was your single chance, girl. Attack a trainer again, and you die for it.' He stalked off.

Pulcher tossed her top to her. 'Back to work. And have more sense in future. If you can!' He was white, and breathing hard.

Cursorily, Divina examined her back. 'Not bad, he go easy, no blood, good, no scar. Learn control! Toss stones, now. Keep up!'

It was silly to resent Divina for holding her − just as well that she had, in fact! Ferocia's malicious slap and insults had started the squabble, but Victoria knew that her own over-reaction had brought the whipping on herself. Now she had to cope with it. She got neither sympathy nor respite for her weals and bruises. She took a furious, defiant satisfaction in keeping her place in the dance. And next time they fenced, she'd drive Ferocia into the dirt!

Two days later Atalanta, excited and apprehensive, pretending confidence for her first fight, joined three other gladiatrixes in a group off to games in Capua. Victoria was calling, 'Good—' when Divina stiff-armed her from behind to stop her. 'Bone-head! No wish good luck! Tempt gods! Say, "Break leg!" '

'Sorry,' Victoria apologised. Every trade had its own customs and superstitions. 'Break a leg, Atalanta!'

Pulcher shut over the door to the exit tunnel. Victoria's back still hurt. Though she couldn't blame him, not really, her smile faded as she turned away.

To her surprise he said, 'Your turn next month, Victrix.' She suspected he was mocking her, but he nodded sourly. 'Every city's holding remembrance games for Nero's baby daughter. And for fun, of course, nothing like seeing people kill each other for having a good time. Six pairs have left already for Antioch, four each for Syracuse and Athens. Become a gladiator and see the world – while you last. Others are going to Capua, Beneventum, other towns nearby. Eight pairs are going to Rome with Glaevius. I'll take you in my team, to the arena here.'

'Really, sir?' She was astonished and pleased. 'I'm that good already?'

A derisive sniff dented her conceit. 'Don't flatter yourself. Everybody's going out who can stand and wave a sword. And we need to discover any cowards or fools, or just unlucky people, before we waste too much time training them.'

Pig! Why was he always so nasty?

Next day, only seven men returned of ten, all of them wounded, and three women. Atalanta's opponent had managed to slash through her net and then her trident after only a short fight.

That evening, as after all games, those who had won spent their two sesterces' earnings on food and wine, to celebrate their survival. Apart from that, though, work went on as before. That was what they were there for, after all.

Victoria went to bed early that night. Alone, she wept quietly for Atalanta. Then she wiped the tears away, before anyone saw and jeered at her, and curled under her blanket. Winter nights were cold, even in Italy. She'd think about that, not about dying.

Who would weep for her?

III

At last, too soon, the day she had longed for arrived; her debut as a gladiatrix.

For the very first time, Victoria put on her fighting clothes. A wide triangle of crimson cloth wrapped round her waist, with the point at the back. The ends tied and tucked in made a thick protective pad high across her belly, below the light leather bodice that showed her midriff to prove she was not wearing body armour. Then the tail was pulled between her legs, up inside the twist, and arranged to hang neatly in front to hide the knot. To keep it all tight and for added protection, a wide, heavy leather belt clipped round the whole bundle of fabric. It was the school's own plain one, for now; she carefully ignored the ominous stains. When – if – no, when! – she grew rich, she could buy her own, as ornate as she liked.

She bent, stretched, twisted, tugged at it. Yes, it all felt firm. She wished she did.

At breakfast, the palaestra was eerily empty. Victoria felt sick, not hungry. The only gladiatrix left, Scythia, was sitting at the rough trestle tables, her broad face with its slanting eyes impassive as usual. 'Eat,' she said. 'You . . .' Her hand made a churning movement in front of her stomach. Victoria nodded.

Scythia grunted. 'Eat. Make better.' Victoria found to her surprise that it wasn't as hard to eat her porridge as she had expected, and it did calm her down.

In the tunnel almost everyone paused to burn a pinch of sweet incense and mutter a prayer to his patron god. Scythia passed by, holding a stone like a spiral shell that hung round her neck, but Victoria made the little sacrifice. 'Bouda, I dedicate to you the blood I may spill. Strengthen my hand, my foot, my heart! And if it is my time to die, make it quick!'

They climbed into a wooden cage built on a cart. 'Now behave yourselves, you rowdy dogs!' Pulcher told them. 'Sit quiet, and don't bark after decent women!'

The men jeered. 'Decent women? In Pompeii? Who're you kidding?'

Grinning, Pulcher locked the cage door and jumped up by the driver. The outer gates opened, and the mules hauled the big cart rumbling out of the tunnel.

Apart from the training runs, this was the first time Victoria had been outside the gates in a month. It was against the law to bury anyone inside a city, so tombs and sepulchres were built along the roads outside the walls. Walking through the necropolis towards the school that first day she had shivered at the ornate tombs and painted statues, like a petrified village. Dead gladiators, like executed criminals, were fed to the city's guard-dogs or the arena beasts, unless they were famous enough to have fans who would pay for their cremation, and for a

plaque or maybe even a statue along here. She'd have a statue
– if she lived long enough . . .

A druid had foretold that she had something important to
do before she died. Not all druids' prophecies came true – ask
Queen Boudicca. Still, it was comforting.

They jolted through the city gate, the cart wheels grinding
in the ruts worn in the stone, between the stepping-stones
that kept pedestrians out of the muck that layered the street
between rainstorms. All market carts and beasts driven to
slaughter had to be off the streets by dawn, but donkeys and
porters laden with baskets and bundles of poultry were still
shoving through the crowds jostling towards the arena.

The narrow streets echoed the rattle of the cart, the braying
and bellowing voices. 'Scented wreaths! Fresh pies, spicy
sausages! Hottest tips for the best fighters! Egyptian perfumes!
Beads, fine beads, glass for your wife, coral for your girlfriend!
Fine wine, only one copper as a cup! Palm-leaf fans! Tell
your fortune, lady? Shady straw hats! Hortensius, fight well, I
adore you! Salted almonds, honey-roast hazelnuts! Look, Dad,
gladiators, an' women! Hi! Good luck!' Victoria touched iron
to deflect the unlucky wish.

The gladiators posed to display their muscles, whistled and
shouted at every woman they saw; Pulcher shook his head in
resignation.

When the cart stopped beside the arena gate, they were led
along a dark tunnel with heavy bolted doors on either side to

a cell with benches along both sides and a small barred window high in the end wall. Victoria was too tense to sit still. She was soon on her feet, pacing about, joking nervously with the other novices. Scythia smiled rather sourly.

The door bolts grated. Pulcher came in, note tablet in hand, peering at the writing on the wax coating inside. 'Here's the programme. The parade, of course. Once round the arena as usual, and back here. Animal fights first, till the crowd fills up. Not a bad list – bears, British hunting dogs, boars, lions with two murderesses, wolves and camels, ostriches for the feathers flying, mounted huntsmen to finish that lot off. Then a break – dancers, music, the stuff the Emperor's trying to replace us with.' Some of the men snarled in disgust.

'Second act – wild horses, twenty hyenas, a bull, and then about thirty criminals with daggers; not just ordinary executions with the criminals tied to stakes for the lions while everybody goes off for lunch, they're making a fight of it. Sort of. Rapists, an arsonist, bad slaves, murderers, the usual assortment, they've been saving up for a good show. Three dangerous crazies who could do anything and might not feel wounds. Heraclitus, Victrix and Tonio, you'll mop up the survivors, whatever they are, with the other novices.'

One of the men grunted, 'Any from Brutus's palaestra? Watch out for a sly slash or trip. "So sorry, pure accident!" But still it slows you down later, when it just might make the difference. Swine.'

'Right, remember it. Keep an eye on them, but watch the criminals first! Another interval to let the crowd piss and buy sweets and drinks, clowns and trick riding, goats on rolling barrels – gods save us! – dancing dogs, fire-eaters, and then the novice fights. Ten pairs of you.' Victoria drew a deep breath. That meant her. 'Don't worry about style, just survive. The important people don't come till later, when the good fighters are on.'

'Huh!' Victoria snorted. 'Thanks.'

'You're welcome.' Wheels squeaked outside. 'Ah, here's our gear.'

Arena slaves wheeled in a trolley laden with their armour and padding. Victoria's fingers felt oddly clumsy as she tied the felt strips round her calves. 'Lower on your right ankle, that'll rub you raw,' Pulcher warned her. He never trusted her to do anything right! But as usual, maddeningly, he was right. She nodded, adjusting it before tying the metal greaves on top.

Scythia and Victoria tied each other's tapes for the felt on their right arms, building a thick pad over the back of the hand and fingers. The smoothly-segmented armour that tied on over it, protecting them from the shoulder down to the wrist, fitted well, and yesterday they had cleaned and oiled it till it moved free as silk. You always saw to your own armour; why trust anyone else with your life?

Today there were plumes, long pheasant feathers to stick in the clips at each side of the high metal ridge on their helmets.

– Victoria had one of the school ones, well polished but nothing as grand as Pulcher's bronze glory, embossed and gilded, with huge red ostrich feathers and a floating horsehair crest. Some day . . .

When they were called at last, Pulcher led them along the tunnel behind the seats towards the sound of music at the Porta Triumphalis, the Gate of Triumph. A dozen fighters in green were coming in from the arena, strutting and waving, then relaxing, taking off their helmets, returning their weapons to a rack under the guards' eyes before heading back to their own rooms. As they passed, they stared in open hostility at Glaevius's team.

'Get your weapons from our rack there,' Pulcher said quietly.

There was Needle! Delighted, Victoria snatched her sword down.

'Careful, it's sharp.'

'Want a shave?' she snapped.

He just sneered. 'Remember, all of you, from now on the blades are real. Helmets on!'

She eased her heavy helmet over her head, to peer through the big round grilles over her eyes. The metal heads turned everyone into sudden goggling strangers. The padding inside would hold it from swivelling, protect her skull and stop the clang deafening her if it was hit. Though it was greasy from all the heads who had worn it before her, the familiar sweaty stink was comforting, and it was so well balanced that it was easy to move in. Its dents reminded her: better to have it than not.

Pulcher settled his own parade helmet, lifted his equally ornate parade shield and sword, and looked round. 'Novices first, in pairs, just follow the editor left. Heads up, wave, brandish your weapons and shields as if you wanted to kill all the magistrates. Ready?' He lifted a hand to the editor, the manager of the games, standing by the gate in his terrifying mask of Rhadamanthus, judge of dead souls. 'Bags of swank! Let's go!'

The sunlight was dazzling after the dim corridors. With flutes, trumpets, drums and the jingle of tambourines, a troupe of musicians and dancing girls and the arena slaves, masked as demons, led the editor and Glaevius's fighters round the fifty-pace-wide circle of raked firm sand. Above the high circling wall and protective netting the expensive, high-class front rows were nearly empty, but beyond them tiers of faces gazed down. When Pulcher appeared, the clapping changed to cheers: 'Pulcher! Pulcher!' Victoria, waving all round, added growing determination to her breathless excitement and nervousness. Some day she would be that famous.

Back in the tunnel, she hung up her sword again and trooped with the rest back to the cell: 'Right, you three. Let me check you over.' Pulcher tightened Victoria's belt till she grunted. 'If your loincloth falls off while you're fighting, the crowd will enjoy it more than you will. Heraclitus, retie your leg padding, it's slack as a circus girl's —' He didn't glance at Victoria, but the next word was lost as he turned round. She almost grinned; as if she didn't often hear that and worse on the palaestra, where the men weren't as mim-mouthed as Pulcher!

The crowd's shouting for the animal hunts drifted in . . .

Too slow, too soon, the door to the tunnel opened again. 'Starters!'

Victoria swallowed as she followed Pulcher out. This was what she wanted.

Wasn't it?

The other novices were already at the gate, armed. She slipped off her head scarf. One heavy-built older man, a slave armed as a secutor, sniggered. 'Who did the fresco on your head, flopsy?' She glared. No; control your temper. She tugged on her helmet, shook her head to settle into the felt padding, and took down Needle. He'd pay for that, sooner or later.

The editor marshalled them into a column of pairs. Heraclitus and Tonio were behind Victoria, at the end. Pulcher nodded to them. 'Don't exhaust yourselves, you'll be on again in an hour. Be ready as soon as the gates open. Victrix, remember, the pointy end. Break a leg, all of you.'

To a blare of trumpets the gates opened and the editor called, 'March on!' As they entered the arena, they lifted their weapons in salute to the magistrates' box where as yet only the chief sponsor of the games sat.

Warily, they spread out, Victoria next to Tonio at the left of the line. Bouda favour her!

All the animals were dead except two hyenas, but most of the criminals were still standing. Several were bleeding. Though badly armed and unarmoured, they still outnumbered the gladiators. Victoria tried to estimate them as she had been taught. They looked scared – not surprising – but the novices had been well warned: even a terrified man will strike, and if he's not trained you have no idea what he'll do. Or several may act together.

One criminal whimpered, abruptly threw down his dagger and fled, while the crowd booed and whistled. The next man, though, snatched it up and raced towards Victoria, a blade in each hand, and all the rest joined the desperate attack. Suddenly, she was faced by four blades, flashing wild and wide.

From her left, Tonio's razor-sharp trident jabbed one man in the neck before he was within arm's length. She knocked his dagger from his hand with her shield on the way to hitting the second man while her armoured right arm fended off a slash from his other knife. Needle lashed aside at the third man, cut his knife hand half off. He screamed, but to her amazement pointed the stump right at her helmet and kept charging, the spurting blood half blinded her, she went down under him, oh Bouda the man with two knives would get her! She scrabbled to escape the third man's desperate hug, his face was pressed against her helmet; she whacked one side of his head with a corner of her shield and the other with Needle's hilt, kicked at the second man under the blades driving for her gut, felt a blade clink on a greave and a sting on her leg, knocked him back a bit, rolled free backwards over her shoulder, nearly cutting her own throat with her sword, thanks for the acrobatics, Pulcher – keep your mind on the job! She reached her feet just in time to fend off two stabs with her shield and her armoured forearm, and strike the second man right in the chest. Needle stuck in his ribs – they'd been warned about that . . . While she tugged to free her sword, the third man, at her feet, grabbed up his dagger with his left hand. He thrust up at her belly, but she arched just far enough away for the point to stop in the thick cloth under her belt, and a couple of frantic blows killed him. *Whoo!*

She glanced round. Tonio was in trouble. He had tripped and trapped one criminal in his net, but the man he had first wounded opposite Victoria had regained his dagger and was attacking. Tonio couldn't let go the net without freeing the man in it, and his other opponent had got inside the strike of the trident and was slashing in messy incompetence at his chest. Victoria jumped forward and struck again. The man dropped. Tonio finished off the one in the net.

Three men were chasing the last hyena round the ring while the crowd yelled in derision and threw fruit at it. The other gladiators were all standing, though some were wounded.

Her first arena fight was over. She was alive and unhurt, apart from a gash on her leg and the bruise from that stab at her stomach. No, it had punctured her, too, but just a nick. Thank Bouda!

Her throat was dry as the arena sand. Drier . . .

'Hey, Tonio, thanks. You're bleeding badly, lean on me.'

'I'll manage,' Tonio panted. 'Thanks to you, too!'

The gladiators paraded round, waving to the crowd. To her surprise, Victoria realised that the clapping grew louder as she passed. They liked her!

From the Porta Libitinensis, the Funeral Door, arena slaves masked to look like Mercury, who guided dead souls to the underworld, were already going round with red-hot irons to check no criminals were faking death to escape, and loading the bodies and the hyenas onto hand-carts. Yoked oxen were stomping in to drag out the horses and the bull, and other slaves were running on with rakes and buckets of sand to cover the blood.

At the Porta Triumphalis, while they hung up their weapons and the surgeon stitched and bandaged Tonio's gashes, all the novices dived for the water jar. 'Three mouthfuls, no more, you'll be sick or bag yourselves up,' Pulcher warned his people. 'You can't move fast with a belly-full of water sloshing about inside you.'

Back in their cell, he shook his head at them. 'Tonio, you've lost blood, so don't show off doing fancy dancy footwork, use your net to trip your man and then get the spikes straight in. Well, Heraclitus. You're limping. You were warned!'

The big lad looked abashed. 'Somebody tripped over one o' them dead dog things, see, an' his shield landed on me heel, see. Were a accident.' He shrugged at Pulcher's disbelieving snort. 'Ain't bad, sir.'

'It'll slow you down. Keep that foot forward as much as you can, less strain on the tendon.' A half-smile twisted Pulcher's mouth as he turned to Victoria. 'And here we have our athletic heroine, Victrix. It's not often the crowd sees someone tumbling like a clown as well as helping a mate.'

She glared at him, wiping blood off her face and helmet. 'What would you have done? Sir? Just let him be killed? He helped me.'

'So he did. If he hadn't, he might not be hurt now. Let it be a lesson to you all. I've never seen that trick with the hand before. Everybody remember it. Victrix, be sure your eyes and your helmet are clean and clear before you go out again.'

Sullenly, she nodded. She had faced three men, and won – but he never praised her.

'Lucky, all of you. In future remember even cheating bank clerks can train in the gymnasium! But next you're fighting fighters. More or less. Some of them may be straight from the slave market. But a couple looked experienced, maybe ex-soldiers, so be ready. As long as you survive, you've done well

– and Glaevius doesn't send out even novices who can't handle a weapon competently.'

The older fighters had heard it all before. 'If you lose, he'll kill you!' one growled, grinning.

When they were called out again, the big secutor bully who had mocked Victoria was already waiting. He snickered at her, 'Mosaic molly! Or is it mould?' as she took off her scarf.

This was not acceptable.

'Can I fight that man, sir?' she whispered to Pulcher, who frowned. Secutor was usually matched against retiarius, not Thracian, and the man was bigger, older, stronger. However, there was no other woman for her to fight; he spoke to the editor. When they were paired off, she found herself next to the oaf. She blew him a kiss, and had the satisfaction of seeing his sneer waver before it was hidden behind his blank metal mask.

They paraded out in style to salute the magistrates, and then marched off to their assigned part of the arena. Her opponent kept hissing a stream of insults and filthy suggestions. 'Stupid cow! Fatso! You ain't a real woman! Ugly savage dolly, I'll skewer you!' He went into obscene detail about how.

He'd not tease her into wild slashing, not that way. She had learned better – thanks, Ferocia! But watch for tricks . . . Sure enough, he pretended to stumble, and his sword would have gashed her leg if she had not been ready to skip nimbly aside.

She saluted him with an extra flourish. From the crowd above her, somebody laughed and clapped.

The fight itself was long enough to worry Victoria. He tried rushing her, but when she avoided him lightly and parried his blows hard enough to jolt his wrist they exchanged blows for quite a while. She was half aware that round her the other fights had finished, and the survivors were standing watching. Tonio was down, and Heraclitus too, sitting looking at his own guts spread over his knees – oh, gods! – Tonio was up again, good – pay attention, before you get your silly head cut off!

At last, though, her heavy-built, heavy-armoured adversary tired, sweating buckets in the noon heat, slowing. She waited for the right moment, ducked left under a heavy swing and leapt in behind his right shoulder, knocked his sword aside as he tried to swipe her back-handed, and thrust at his side. He managed to deflect Needle with his armoured elbow, but it sent him off balance. He staggered sideways, she slipped a foot between his ankles and hit him with her shield, and he fell, twisting to get his big shield over him like a turtle's shell. The temptation was irresistible; she sat down astride it.

He heaved, trying to toss her off. 'Lie still, you!' she yelled, pounding his helmet with Needle's hilt in high excitement. 'Or I'll cut your fool head off! Surrender! Ask for mercy!'

There was nothing else he could do. His helmet waggled. 'Let me up, then,' he mumbled.

'So you can go on fighting? I'm not that stupid a cow! You can get a hand up from there!'

He dropped his sword and waved urgently. Victoria, still sitting on him, grinning inside her helmet, also raised a hand to the crowd, and was delighted to see them waving to her to let the oaf live.

As she stood up to let him rise, it dawned on her that there was a lot of laughter round her. She looked round. The surviving novices had removed their helmets and were guffawing, even the wounded ones. Above her, the people in the seats were rolling about laughing, clapping, some actually tossing flowers towards the arena for her. They did like her!

Pulcher had said to stay incognito, keep her head hidden for now, but she was stifled. Besides, he wasn't out here, he didn't feel the crowd's approval; she was, she did. She reached up and tugged off the heavy helmet, shook her head to get rid of the fug of steam, relished the gasp and shout above her as they took in the colours of her scalp. Triumphantly, she lifted Needle in her right hand, her helmet and her shield in her left, shrieked an ecstatic war-cry, and gloried in the cheering.

She had done it! She was a gladiatrix!

IV

After only three fights as a novice, Victoria was promoted to the afternoon combats, when the rich and powerful, the magistrates and merchants, bankers and senators on holiday, arrived to lounge in the shade of the new saffron-yellow awnings over the arena and bet on the real fighters.

Soon she persuaded Glaevius to let her wear her Iceni clothes, just for an experiment, though Pulcher objected – trust him! She felt smugly pleased when the crowd went wild, and she was allowed to continue with them. A fan club developed, a group of rich young men – and some flashy females, too, in the women's rows high at the back – who screamed in adulation and began to join in when she swept off her helmet and shouted her war-cry after winning. Graffiti appeared by the palaestra gate: 'Ah, Victrix, you have conquered my soul!' and such like. She loved it!

Editors began to ask for her as an individual, not just as part of a set. Her hire price, she discovered with pride, was very high for such a newcomer to the arena. She got cocky, and won herself another whipping for impertinence.

Around her, the fighters came and went, were bought or

joined them. Several novices died, like Atalanta and Heraclitus, in their first fight. They were never more than fifteen women, with maybe another ten in other schools. Gladiatrixes were rare.

Big Gallia caught the summer marsh fever and couldn't throw it off. Glaevius finally put her out, with ten silver sesterces. She started a pie shop near the school gate, doing quite well with people holding funeral feasts in the necropolis, but was attacked by robbers and killed six months later. Alexandria, the huge black woman, gained an admirer, a Greek nobleman, who bought her out.

A wild Spanish girl, newly bought in, attacked a trainer and was crucified on the wall at the end of the palaestra. The horrible death, so much worse than the normal arena death that they were all used to, chilled the school's mood for a month. Another girl was caught stealing; she suffered the usual punishment: running the gauntlet between all the gladiators in two lines, armed with belts and spear shafts, and died. Ferocia, to no-one's regret, was killed – not in the arena, but in a fight over a man. Unfortunately she killed the other woman too, who was much better liked.

One day when ten gladiatrixes were sent on against a hippopotamus, a new girl was bitten in half and another two trampled to death before they finally managed to kill the four-ton, armour-plated monster with the arm-long teeth, in a ghastly, bloody shambles. Victoria thought herself lucky to escape with a broken arm. Glaevius left the hunts to the expert huntsmen in future.

Africa received a nasty stab in her knee, but healed to fight again before Glaevius lost patience. She and Hippolyta completed their contracts. Hippolyta left to become a decorative private bodyguard, which broke Thraex's heart; she was killed in her next fight. Africa signed on again for better conditions, a room of her own and freedom to go out as she pleased after training, as Divina did. Scythia was so badly wounded that though the crowd gave her mercy, Manny could not save her.

After sixteen fights, Victoria had eleven scars from combat and twenty-one from training accidents. Her popularity grew so great that the crowd would grant mercy to her opponent whenever she asked for it, so that she had only four times had to dispatch a beaten fighter. Though the first time the woman was so badly wounded she would probably have died soon anyway, Victoria moped afterwards until her comrades mocked her, and Divina scolded her for arguing with fate. She pulled herself together; yes, it was the worst bit of the job, but it had to be done. The second was a man, a coward; she had no compunction about sending him to the underworld.

The one time she was beaten, by a thrust in the side from Achillidus – shorter but stronger and equally fast, and more experienced, the star of another school – the crowd was waving for mercy before she even raised a hand.

'Anyone kills you, I think the crowd would lynch them,' Achillidus muttered, helping Victoria to stand and supporting her while beckoning the attendants.

'Good to know I've got friends,' Victoria grunted.

'You threw me eye off with that dive forward. Nearly gutted me, too.'

'I skidded, blood under the sand.'

Achillidus snorted as he lowered Victoria to a stretcher. 'Lucky bitch.'

Yes, she thought; Bouda was looking after her. So far.

Victoria was almost the only person on her palaestra who could read. When love letters and poems arrived for the others, she had always read them out to amuse everybody. Then they started to come for her: 'Victrix, come and fight with me, Victrix, Victrix, please agree, If your sword should ever miss, You could slay me with a kiss!' That got her a lot of teasing: 'Try slayin' me wi' a kiss, Victrix – ye'll get somethin' ye didn't bargain for in return!'

Presents arrived, too: flowers, fruit, suggestive statuettes, jewellery – only glass beads at first, but soon coral and pearls, a silver bracelet and a good onyx intaglio seal of a gladiator. Clothes – bright tunics, embroidered scarves – with notes: 'Wear this, and you wear my heart!' Occasionally a purse was delivered: 'You won me ten thousand sesterces, so I send you my thanks. Keep it up!'

Glaevius started entering her for individual contests with

money prizes, not just wreaths. Though on his advice she banked some of her share of the money, she argued, 'I might not live to spend it later,' and had new clothes made, both for the arena and finery for outside, for she developed a social life.

After six months volunteers could go out occasionally after training, with permission. Victoria enjoyed sailing downriver to the Middle Sea on the barges that brought up goods from the coastal wharves. She made a small donation towards rebuilding the temple of Venus, the patron goddess of the town, after the big earthquake a couple of years before. In the women's side of the baths she luxuriated in a good hot sweat and scrape-down – a Roman habit she eagerly adopted.

Everywhere she was enthusiastically recognised, greeted with gifts and good wishes. Fresco painters let her try her hand at flowers and fruit, and uncomplaining either cut it out and redid it or, if the house owner preferred, left her work to stand, triumphantly signed 'Victrix!' The builders repairing the earthquake-tossed columns round the forum showed her how to plaster the brick cores with stucco, a mix of bright marble dust and cement to imitate marble, and made her decorative plaques to hang in the dormitory. Tailors hunted out their brightest cloths, and ordered more from Gaul for her. She was offered fruit and snacks, and more wine than she wanted, for the publicity value of having her eat at a stall.

Several times she was hired to do display fights at big dinner parties. Once was against a leopard – chained. She didn't have to kill it, just put on an exciting show with a trick sword that squirted fake blood. Its claws weren't fake, though, and she nearly lost a hand. She usually stayed afterwards for an hour to be feted by the guests.

Then, one day, an invitation arrived simply to dinner, not to fight. To the house of one of the richest bankers in the town.

The women who were regularly invited out offered advice.

'You can't wear your arena gear! They'll think you're just a savage,' Africa protested, her dark skin exotic against ochre yellow and gold.

Divina, delicate in her favourite frilly pink, spat indelicately in the dust and disagreed. '*Tchah!* Wear what you like, girl! But make them respect you, get good gifts.' She winked. 'Take gifts, have fun. But keep cold inside, remember, no tangle, or lose sharp, lose life.'

Victoria chuckled. 'Don't worry, Divina, I'll never get serious about any man. And Africa, they can take me as I am, me, the British fighter, or do without me! I'm me, I'm different! I'm the cousin of a king!'

Passing by, Pulcher jeered, 'In Britain kings are like cocks, one on every dunghill. Every beggar and his dog's a king's cousin.' Victoria thumbed her nose at him – behind his back.

She decided on a long-sleeved shirt in red-and-green tartan, striped blue-and-black trousers, a silvery wolf-hide jerkin with the head snarling behind the shoulders – sweltering in summer heat, but worth it – and a long red cloak with a trim of white winter hare fur. Pulcher hid his eyes, pretending to be dazzled. 'By Hercules, we'll not lose you in a crowd.'

Divina showed her how to use eyeliner, rouge on her lips and cheeks and earlobes, blue paint on her eyelids. When Victoria studied the result in Divina's mirror, she thought she looked stunning, but Pulcher sneered. 'You look ridiculous. A cross between an African idol and an Egyptian pleasure-girl.'

'I paint so!' Divina protested.

'That's what I mean! Get it off!'

Divina laughed. Victoria didn't. Huffily, she wiped her face, leaving only the merest trace. In the palaestra she must obey Pulcher, but why outside?

An hour before sunset, on her way to the gate, Glaevius stopped her. 'Victrix. A warning. Popidius Ampliatus and his friends see themselves as connoisseurs of the finer points of combat while they lounge on cushions and nibble honey-roasted almonds. Most get a thrill simply by being so close to someone, especially a woman, who actually does the fighting.' He sniffed in contempt. 'However, in his house he may want more. You will refuse.'

She had no intention of romping like Divina. 'Of course, sir.'

Perhaps she had sounded huffy. He sighed. 'What I mean is that if Ampliatus, or one of his guests, thinks it would be amusing to fight you, you will refuse. You are strictly forbidden to fight, even with wooden swords, except on my orders. If they want a display combat, they must hire you. What else you do, or refuse to do, I do not care. Just remember that these men pay for the games. Ampliatus is having the Temple of Isis repaired at his own expense, but in the name of his son, to get the brat onto the Town Council even though he is only six. That is how wealthy he is. Do not offend him.'

Her reply was demure. 'Yes, sir. I mean no, sir. Gentle as a goldfish, that's me.'

He was surprised into a bark of laughter, though as usual his face remained immobile. 'That I'll not demand of you. Be cold and scaly as you like. But remember, you are legally a slave. If you strike a free man, you can be flogged. Use a weapon, and you will be crucified. Offend Ampliatus, and he might tell the games editors not to give me contracts, which could ruin me. So be careful!'

Pulcher waylaid her in the tunnel out. 'I'll come to collect you an hour before midnight. Be ready. If I have to come in for you, both you and your host will find it embarrassing.'

'Yes, sir.' She felt furiously insulted. He seldom showed his face to invite mockery outside the palaestra. Why now? Did he think she couldn't take care of herself? He was so arrogant, so offensive, especially to her for some reason, however hard she worked to please him. Why did so many rich ladies want to visit him? Though he was not bad-looking. Odd, nowadays she never noticed his scars.

★ ★ ★

She found her host's house easily enough, not far from the forum, where the house steward scolded her. 'You're late! What kept you?'

Fuss-pot! 'Did Ampliatus want me to come all sweaty and gritty from training?'

He sniffed. 'Yes, I mean no, well, I suppose – Myron, take her right in! Haven't those musicians arrived yet? And the asparagus . . .' He flurried off.

The boy Myron simply jerked his head at Victoria to follow him, but she grabbed his ear. '*Hoy.*' He yelped; her fingers were strong. 'My cloak?'

An elegant slave stepped forward disdainfully. At Victoria's glower his expression smoothed. Victoria tossed him her cloak. 'Right, Myron. Lead on!' Grimly she marched after the boy. If anyone else looked down his nose at her, he'd find it rearranged, and to Hades with what Glaevius had said!

No; calm, control.

Through a hall where half-clad statues swarmed like a bathhouse, every corner barnacled with gilded twiddles, she was led to a dining-room whose red walls had the newest style of fresco panels showing frenzied cock and dog-fights. Not good for the digestion, she thought. Slaves glided round the open central area, keeping wine cups filled for the nine men who lay on couches round it, each with a pretty young man or woman sitting beside him.

As she paused in the doorway, the men noticed her. 'She's here! Victrix!'

On the central couch Popidius Ampliatus raised a beringed hand and superciliously beckoned her to approach. Someone called, 'Victrix! Victrix!' and they all took up the chant, clapping in time to her steps, making it a triumphal march. Pleased, she stepped short to make it last longer.

Ampliatus lifted his gilded red glass cup to her. 'Greetings, Victrix, conqueror of the ring!' His fleshy, dark-jowled face was familiar; it often stared down at her from the magistrates' seats, surrounded by young men. He always dressed in the latest fashions, trying to convince everybody, including himself, that he was still one of the lads, young and virile. He was wrong. A little bald patch peeped coyly through his marigold wreath, and Victoria hid a grin while everybody cheered, rolling on their cushion-crammed couches to raise their cups to her.

He patted the couch beside his head. 'Join me.'

Stiffening slightly, she perched beside him. Like the painted pleasure girls – Pulcher had been right about the make-up, curse him! Did Ampliatus think . . . ? Yes. His hand clamped on her thigh.

Firmly Victoria removed it. 'Your invitation to dinner is an honour and a pleasure, Popidius Ampliatus.' She smiled at him sweetly – and briefly. Would he take the hint?

No. His hand returned to her leg.

Right, it would have to be said straight out. She looked at him, slitty-eyed. 'I was invited for dinner, sir. That only.'

His eyebrows rose in mocking surprise. 'A woman of virtue, eh? Oh, Victrix! You must be the only one in Pompeii!'

She grinned tightly at him. 'You sound just like the blokes on the palaestra.' As his jaw dropped slightly – what impertinence, to compare him with such scum! – she removed his hand again, gripping hard enough to make him wince. 'If I'm the only one in Italy, it makes no difference. I am what I am, and that's no ripe peach for plucking.'

'*O-ooh!* Cheeky!' But he seemed to accept it, and waved for the meal to begin.

Right through the first course – oysters and other shellfish, crayfish and lobster, snails in garlic and deliciously crisp salads – he and his friends orated about the arts of the arena, and great fighters of the past. They neither wanted nor expected her to comment, which suited her. Talking shop with civilians bored her.

The band entered as the second course was carried in. Ampliatus described all the delicacies, and how much they and the plates they came on cost: the roast sow with her suckling piglets arranged beside her, each with a different stuffing and sauce; the geese, ducks, herons; the baked porpoise; the pies of larks' tongues; the boiled calf; the skewers of singing birds, thrushes, fig-peckers, blackbirds; the roasted roe deer; the asparagus, which had finally arrived . . .

Each guest reclined on his left elbow, supported by cushions. The escorts actually fed their hosts, picking titbits from the platters that the slaves brought round and stuffing them into the open mouths, like mother birds feeding their young. There was a lot of giggling. Victoria felt rather disgusted.

Popidius Ampliatus saw her face. 'Your people don't do this, Victrix?'

'We teach our children to feed themselves.'

Her host repeated the joke loudly for everyone; the guests hooted with laughter, the attendants giggled charmingly.

With the third course – trays of fruit, cakes and tarts – a vast pie with a high, gilded crust was carried in. 'Ah! Get ready!' All the escorts jumped up, clapping their hands and squealing in childish anticipation. Embarrassing, Victoria thought.

No; like herself they were professionals. They all did what the employer expected. Whatever their private feelings, they giggled, she fought. Their job was easier, but Victoria preferred hers.

At Ampliatus's nod, the carver plunged a huge knife into the crust, releasing a flight of white doves. The escorts ran and leapt to chase the birds, shrieking in glee, draperies flying, while the men cheered them on. 'Each bird carries a token for a prize, you see,' Popidius Ampliatus explained.

When all the birds were caught, the tokens were brought forward. Some prizes were pleasant, like the tiny monkey, or the bracelet of seven agates. However, two very dead rats were solemnly presented amid huge hilarity. One flabbergasted winner demanded, 'What can you do with six camels?' Most of the suggestions were rude or physically impossible, or both. When the girl who won eight painted eggs lifted one, it broke in her hands. It was full of perfume. Laughing, she tossed one onto each couch – and to guffaws d shrieks found that two were simply rotten eggs.

'Four hundred sesterces' worth of perfume!' Popidius Ampliatus boasted.

Politely, Victoria smiled. 'We eat more simply in Britain. Even in the king's house.'

'You've eaten with a king? Even a British one?'

No, but she wasn't going to admit it. 'I'm the cousin of a king! But this feast is – amazing.'

He waved a dismissive hand. 'Adequate for a few friends, though not for anyone really important, of course.' Oh, thank you, she thought. Was the insult intentional, or teasing, or just unthinking arrogance? He chuckled fatly. 'You're better off here. Not many feasts in Britain these days, even for cousins of kings.'

Some of the men had gone to empty their bellies or bowels into pots behind a screen in one corner, and then returned to their couches to call for their favourite dishes to be brought back, or just to paw the escorts. Ampliatus's hand slid again onto Victoria's leg. She removed it again. 'No.'

He smirked, his marigold wreath slipping over one eye. 'You're a slave –'

'Not your slave. I obey Glaevius and his trainers, and nobody else. But what was that about no feasts in Britain?'

'Ah, yes. You've heard of the barbarian queen's revolt, haven't you?' He sneered. 'What a harpy, eh? But stupid. How she could dream of defying Rome—'

Victoria bristled. 'She burned three towns, and wiped out a legion – not bad for a barbarian! About the feasts?'

'What? Oh. No, Victrix. The lack of them! General Suetonius has burned all Britain's houses and crops, executed hundreds, sent thousands as slaves back to the markets here. They're all starving, dying, they'll never rise again! A thorough lesson!'

Ampliatus might be a successful banker, but as a person he was loathsome.

'Cheer up, I've a little something for you, too!' Victoria sat rigid as he pushed himself up on one arm and gestured to the steward to call for silence. 'Victrix, wonderful Victrix!' Everybody cheered. 'Your skill in the arena is matchless!' More cheers. 'We all admire you.' Cheers again. This was what they liked when they were full; simple, straightforward, nothing to strain the brain. 'We applaud you.' They did. 'We love you! We worship you! So we offer you tribute. From your own country, from Britain itself! Royal tribute for the brilliant queen of the ring! Listen, everyone – Victrix is the cousin of a king!'

While they all laughed, the steward brought forward a red silk cushion with a gold necklace; a slim C-shape of twisted gold, ending in gold knobs. A torc.

Victoria's strained smile faded. A torc ripped from some warrior noble in Britain, dead or enslaved or simply robbed. Maybe even her own father.

The guests shouted drunken applause. 'Incredible generosity! Astonishing! So appropriate! Savage splendour! Exquisite taste!'

While they were praising Ampliatus, they were sneering at her. Victoria felt like killing her host, and all of them. No; control . . .

She accepted the torc, to save its honour. She had to show him how it was twisted open and squeezed on. It felt slimy, as if his hands had left slug trails on it. She even managed a few words of thanks.

A troupe of Spanish dancers appeared. Amid the cheering and fuss and the blatter of guitars and tambourines, she slipped away.

Outside in the hallway she stopped, rigid in distress. If she had been alone, not out in public among hurrying slaves, she would have burst into tears. Control . . .

Her family – her Iceni family. Her uncle and aunt, her cousin, her friends . . . What had happened to them? She had been so busy, so childishly excited in her new life that she had forgotten them.

The heartbreaking memory of proud Boudicca's death

swept over her. The queen's whisper echoed in her mind: 'As ruthlessly as they destroy my people, your people, so you will destroy them.' Rome was destroying Britain, as the queen had feared. So it was her duty, her sacred duty, to destroy Rome. That was why she had come here. Becoming a gladiatrix was only one step on the path.

Her knuckles whitened on the torc. This was no coincidence. This was a message from the gods. They had inspired this arrogant Roman to give it to her, to recall her to her obligation. She would remember from now on.

A hand on her arm made her jump. Popidius Ampliatus smirked at her, the doors to the dining room wide open behind him so that everyone could watch. 'Now, now, mustn't run away! I expect thanks for the present, my dear. A good deal of thanks!' His arm snaked round her waist, his heavy lips reached greedily for her face – Then his eyes crossed, he rose to his toes with a whimper.

In the interested hush all around, Victoria eased her grip. 'I warned you, no.' She hesitated. Don't offend him? A bit late for that. But . . . save his face. His back was to the dining room door. 'Why not tell your friends that you let me go home now as a gesture of sympathy – I lost my family in the rebellion and was upset at being reminded of it? They'll praise your kindness as well as your generosity.' She carefully avoided sneering. 'And, er, I do thank you.' She hadn't really hurt him . . .

Her cloak was tenderly wrapped round her shoulders at the front door; she did not notice the slaves' usually wooden faces glowing with unspoken glee.

When three men jumped out to rob this stupid woman walking alone in the dark, quite automatically she used two fast wrestling moves to dislocate the arm of one and seize his cudgel. Then she stared at them so blankly, so clearly unimpressed and unafraid, that they backed away in awe: 'She's a ghost, or a demon!'

At the city gate the guard recognised her, but at the bleakness of her face in the light of their lantern they opened the postern for her without a word. Silently she strode on among the silent tombs that exactly matched her mood.

When she knocked at the school gate, Pulcher opened it. About to express surprise at her early return, he looked more closely, wordlessly led Victoria inside and laid his lantern down on the shelf of the shrine behind him. 'Ampliatus gave you trouble?' His voice was astonishingly gentle. The candlelight outlined the curve of his jaw, the curl of his hair.

'No.' She was almost brisk. 'I – convinced him to leave me alone.'

Pulcher glanced down at the cudgel she still held. 'With that?'

She blinked at it in mild wonder, and tossed it aside. 'No. More – personally . . .' As he chuckled quietly, she opened her cloak to show him the gleam of gold at her throat. 'And he gave me a fine present.'

He studied the torc. 'British?' His eyes flicked to the strain on her face. 'Memories.'

Somehow that started her tears. She wept silently, deep, shuddering sobs; and he held her tight, his arms firm and comforting round her shoulders, murmuring, 'It's all right, it's all right.'

After only a moment, she managed to control herself. What an exhibition to make of herself! She shoved him away. 'I'm all right. Just tired.'

'If you're sure—'

Patronising pig! 'Of course I'm sure! Just leave me alone!'

He drew back and mutely ushered her across the yard to her dormitory.

V

For days Victoria could scarcely bear to look Pulcher in the face, after that disgracefully soppy exhibition at the gate. He never referred to it, though he was more sarcastic and critical than usual. Gradually it faded from her mind.

She quickly became as fashionable a dinner guest as Divina and Africa. The dandies who idolized her nearly all tried to make love to her, taking her steady refusal as a challenge. She discovered, in amused contempt, that some were actually boasting about their bruises. However, finally their advances faded, became only a formal gesture, and she could relax and enjoy herself – up to a point. Most of the people who were thrilled by her as by a leopard on a chain were fatuous, arrogant slugs, even those who prided themselves on being athletic. She despised them.

Constantly nowadays she remembered her mission. Every scrap of information she heard about Britain confirmed the devastation that the Romans had made of her country, and strengthened her conviction that in return she must somehow destroy the great city, the capital of the world: Rome.

Her, one girl, alone? Absurd! Certainly; but still, she must try. But how?

Fighting in the arena she could kill only slaves. She needed to reach Rome itself, the senators, the government, the Emperor. But how?

One day a scented little scroll was delivered. 'Pretty . . . Oh, it's not another poem. An invitation to call tomorrow afternoon, from a woman for a change. No, not an invitation – a summons! Julia Felix. I know a Marcus Julius Felix. A relation?'

'Julia Felix?' Divina's jaw dropped. 'Richest woman in Pompeii!'

Glaevius was puzzled. 'Julia Felix is not noble, Victrix, only equestrian class, but very influential, an old flame of Emperor Claudius and many of the senators. Retired now, and rigidly respectable. Everybody in the government knows her, her daughters and Nero's new wife Poppaea took dancing classes together. The gods know why she should be interested in an uncultured savage!'

Pulcher looked wry; 'Glaevius says she might ask you to stay for dinner.' He sniffed. 'That is, frankly, as likely as to see her singing in the streets for coppers. However, if she *should* feel like slumming, I don't expect her dinners will run late, but he says tonight you can stay out as late as you like. I don't. Midnight.'

She grinned. 'I'd love to see you push your way in there to collect me!'

'Don't make it necessary.' His voice was cold.

He probably would, too, Bouda take him!

Waves and good wishes from passers-by who recognised Victoria, to her never-fading delight, surrounded her as she passed the high-class shops selling pearls and perfumes and silks, crossed the forum, and walked down the Via Abbondata to the older, less fashionable end near the arena. The big house was perfectly repaired and replastered in blue and white stucco, better than Ampliatus's had been and months ahead of the forum; a sign of the lady's power in the town.

A neat, elderly steward bowed to her. 'Welcome to the house of Julia Felix, Miss Victrix. Would you care to rinse your feet, refresh yourself? No? Then be pleased to follow me. The mistress is in the garden.'

Polite. Good.

This was different from the opulence of Ampliatus's house or the vast villas outside the town that she had visited before. These walls had old-fashioned frescoes, airy panels of gardens, flowers and birds, and exquisite portrait mosaics, so fine and delicate that her thumbnail would cover twenty tiles. No bloodthirsty hunts or sweaty fighters here, and very little gilding. Even as an uncultured savage, she recognised restrained wealth and refined taste when she saw it. Niches held Greek and Egyptian vases, flowers, or superb statuettes and bronzes, perhaps relics of the lady's flighty past.

The steward led her through an archway curtained with tinkling green glass beads, out into the main garden of sweet-scented flowers. Marble colonnades shading doorways surrounded a pool. Victoria loathed fountains like this, a fat little boy squeezing a dolphin till it vomited. She grinned to herself at the defiant thought; even an uncultured savage need not be totally overwhelmed by all this aristocratic elegance.

In the shade of a vine-covered pergola a severe old lady was sitting very upright in a wickerwork chair. Her dull wine-red gown matched the glow of the rounded rubies in her ears and the pins that held her high-plaited white hair. She looked as if Victoria was something smelly that the dog had dragged in.

'The gladiatrix Victrix. I have heard of you, of course.'

No welcome here. Snooty old biddy, sneering like a horse in a huff! Right; Victoria would act equally formal and haughty. She just wished her new clothes were a little less vivid – no, she didn't! She was cousin to a king! She bowed. 'I am honoured by your attention, Julia Felix.'

The silence lengthened awkwardly.

Victoria was opening her mouth to comment nervously on the beautiful garden, the elegant house, anything, when she saw the contempt in Julia Felix's eyes. The old gorgon was trying to set her off balance, gain an advantage, like getting the sun in your eyes in the arena. Whatever your opponent wants, you don't give him. Or her. Her eyes slitting slightly, Victoria shut her mouth again, lifted her chin, relaxed her shoulders and stood still, on parade. Control. Bags of swank . . .

Her hostess's thin lips pursed, showing just a hint of surprised, reluctant appreciation. 'I believe you know my grandson.'

'A courteous, intelligent young man,' Victoria nodded. Of course, that was why she had been asked here. Her own lips tightened. 'Let me save time and reassure you, lady. I am not looking for a rich husband or lover. Many of your grandson's friends give me gifts. Julius Felix gave me a pair of coral earrings last month when he won a bet on me. But I don't ask for anything from any of them. They invite me to parties. The cooking's better than on the palaestra, and there's often music, which I enjoy. I always leave early.'

She leaned forward. 'Look, lady. I'm no gold-digger, nor any ripe fruit for picking. I want to become a great fighter. In my homeland that is considered deeply honourable. I'll not do anything to put that at risk. I work hard, very hard, with Pulcher and the other trainers, and risk my life in the arena. I can't do that if I become drunken or debauched or idly pleasure-seeking. If you object to your grandson knowing such a low character as a gladiatrix, don't tell me. Tell him to avoid me. I'll not chase him, nor complain.'

Julia Felix hummed doubtfully, but then, to Victoria's surprise, nodded grudging approval. 'I am relieved. My grandson's recent friends are – inappropriate. Noisy, brash, dissolute. Vulgar.' Her tone was blighting.

Hiding a smile, Victoria nodded agreement. 'Wild. Very like the young warriors of my own tribe back in Britain, lady.'

To Victoria's wry amusement, Julia Felix looked insulted; no Roman citizen could accept a comparison between Roman citizens and savages. 'My grandson is . . .' She hesitated.

A hanger-on at the back of the group; weak. 'Impressionable?' Victoria offered.

The old lady sniffed scathingly. 'Weak, you mean. Less backbone than a jellyfish. His father never beat him enough.' It was Victoria's turn to be surprised. 'Such raffish company will damage his reputation, as well as ruining what little character he has. And he will soon start to ascend the course of honour.'

She raised a patronising eyebrow at Victoria's blank expression. 'You don't understand? No, you're from Britain, and low-class.'

Well, thank you, Victoria thought; from this lady, that was cheeky. But through her beauty and brains Julia Felix had done extremely well for herself; she'd be impressed even less than Pulcher had been by a relationship with a British king.

'The course of honour is the traditional career path for a young man of good family' – noticing Victoria's eyebrows twitch, she slipped in, stiffly – 'like my grandson – my older daughter married a senator's younger son.' With the help of a gigantic dowry, Victoria guessed, and bowed respectfully. 'He will spend some years in the army as a tribune, a junior officer. At the right age, he will enter the senate, and seek election through all the government posts, learning how the Empire is run. Quaestor, seeing to taxes and money supply, then aedile, running a city's police, firemen, markets, and so on. Praetor, an advocate and judge in the law courts. He may be asked to join the staff of a general, or assist a provincial governor for a while in any of these posts. When he is well-known and popular, he may seek election as consul, the highest post in Rome – under the Emperor, of course.'

Her lips tightened. Victoria realised that at that point the plan might come apart; her hostess's wealth, however lavishly spent on gladiatorial games and parties, presents and bribes, might not be quite enough to outweigh the disadvantage to her grandson of her low birth and risqué past.

'Consulars – that means ex-consuls, girl – are sent out as governors and procurators to the provinces, where a clever man can make his fortune.'

Victoria nodded. 'Catus Decianus started the rebellion in Britain by trying to grab a whole tribe's wealth for himself – for Nero, he said, but how much would have reached Rome?'

Julia Felix stiffened again at the criticism of a Roman. 'A disgraceful affair, a total waste of money and lives. How dared they!'

'Yes indeed, lady.' Victoria hid her sudden furious resentment. 'Greedy and brutal, all the Roman officials.'

The old lady blinked. 'The tribes! And that viper queen, Bondicia.' Victoria smiled slightly. Julia Felix lowered her chin and regarded her with more attention. 'You knew what I meant.' Victoria's smile widened. 'Perhaps I should revise my opinion of gladiators' intelligence.' Julia Felix's voice was a shade less chilly. She gestured frail fingers towards a second chair.

Victoria sat, politely veiling her triumph. She had won the snobby old bitch's respect at last!

Perhaps it was that unexpected esteem that made the old lady go on talking. 'You mentioned Pulcher. A young man with terrible scars on his face?'

'Yes, lady.'

'Such a pity. A striking little boy.'

Victoria could scarcely believe it. 'You know him, lady?'

Julia Felix lifted a negative hand. 'I knew his family. You don't know the story?' As Victoria shook her head, trying not to look too eager, the old lady seemed pleased, whether she took a delight in malicious gossip or was simply glad to have a new face to talk to even if it was a gaudy low-class barbarian.

'You know a senator who has no sons often adopts one from a good family that has too many. As our own Emperors have done for five generations.'

Victoria's eyebrows twitched. The lady's dry tone was

dangerous! The Emperor had spies everywhere, they said. Though a lady as well-connected as Julia Felix must surely be safe . . .

'That is what happened to your Pulcher. His adoptive father – call him Publius, it is not his name – he had no child. Prayers, sacrifices, two new wives – nothing worked. In desperation, Publius adopted the younger son of one of his cousins, a child of about ten – handsome, mannerly, intelligent, ideal – to make him his heir. But Marina, Publius's third wife, had been ill and lost the beauty he had married her for. He planned to divorce her, and marry again – my younger daughter, as it happens. However, Marina learned his plan. It meant disaster for her. She was neither rich nor, nowadays, beautiful enough to attract another husband. She would have to go and live with her brother and his wife, the meanest couple in Italy, and help look after their six children. Her life would have been wretched. So' – she drew a deep breath – 'Marina waited until the adoption was complete, all the papers signed, no chance of cancelling it, and then went into the boy's room one night with a razor and – *slash*! What an heir for Publius to present to his friends! Then poor Marina returned calmly to her own room and killed herself. Such a scandal! I refused to allow my daughter to be linked with it.'

Victoria ignored that rather hypocritical comment; she was horrified. 'But what about the boy? Didn't she consider him at all?'

'The boy?' Julia Felix looked rather surprised. 'I shouldn't think so. It ruined his life, of course. When they realised how hideous he was always going to be, Publius refused ever to see him again. As soon as he became legally an adult at fourteen, the lad walked out and joined Glaevius. He said, I'm told, that since he was considered a disgraceful public spectacle he'd do it thoroughly. At least he did not shame either of his families by using their name.'

Victoria was breathless. Even the insults from the old lady were worth it. What a story! Wouldn't the others be enthralled? Poor child, his life must have been a misery. Her heart actually hurt with the unexpected force of her pity.

At the green curtain, the steward coughed gently. 'My lady, two friends from Rome. Will I show your visitor out?' He raised a disparaging eyebrow towards Victoria, who bristled at the implied insult. But Julia Felix might be embarrassed, and however high-nosed she was, the old biddy didn't deserve that. Victoria rose to leave.

The steward jumped aside as a small man brushed nimbly through the curtain past him. His pock-marked, raddled face could have been any age from thirty-five to sixty; his hair was too golden and his wide, lively lips too pink to be true.

Victoria withdrew as far as she could behind a cypress, meaning to slip away unnoticed.

The visitor dropped his purple-edged senator's toga like a rag, revealing a long dark green tunic with shocking gilt scalloped fringes, and skipped forward to kneel dramatically at Julia Felix's feet, seize and kiss her hands. 'Wine! Wine! Darling Julia Felix, a fountainful of your fabulous frosted Falernian, before my fiery froat fries to a frazzle!'

Julia Felix frowned and smiled, shaking her head like an aunt reproving a favourite nephew. 'You didn't carry any with you?'

'But of course!' He looked scandalized. 'We drank it, dear!' Slaves were already bringing in wine, nibbles and extra seats. He seized a glass in each hand, drank deep and sighed voluptuously. 'A-ah! Just in time! I can feel my little limp tendrils stiffening up again nicely!' Tossing aside the glasses – the servants, alert, leapt to catch them – he clasped his hands as if in prayer. 'In the name of Aesculapius, darling, you simply must give me sanctuary!'

He turned, caught sight of Victoria, and stopped short, hands raised, gilded fingernails glinting in the sunshine, gazing with dropped jaw. 'But who, my dear, who is this gorgeously exotic creature?'

Exotic? Who . . . ? Victoria actually turned to see who was behind her, before she realised he meant her. Exotic! She couldn't slip away now. But he was amusing, and it wasn't her fault she'd been seen. She stood still, trying not to blush as the man rose gracefully to examine her from tattooed scalp to crimson sandals. Julia Felix's tight-cornered mouth showed irritated resignation.

He sighed in affected rapture. 'Oh, Hermes Trismegistus! Why did I ever think that Rome was the only place to find enchantment? Caenis! Caenis, where are you? Caenis, come along, do, and see what a wonderful, wonderful surprise lovely Julia Felix has for us! It's a young goddess! Or a titan, maybe? Definitely not a nymph, far too solid and earthy, and brilliantly bi–ig! But much too colourful for one of the frowsty old fogeys up on Olympus!'

The steward held back the bead curtain to let another lady enter the garden. Caenis was short and slender, not young nor particularly beautiful, but her dark eyes were intelligent. Her smoothly plaited hairstyle and amber jewellery, her gown of soft bronze veiling over chestnut silk were all simple, elegant; Victoria felt suddenly sorry for Divina and her gaudy rose-pinks. The lady was shaking her head in exasperation. 'Don't be so silly, Petronius! He's been like this all the way, Julia Felix.'

'I can't help it! It's the fresh air, dear – and freedom!' Petronius protested.

Not noticing Victoria, Caenis sighed as if at a naughty child. 'I'm sorry for landing on you without warning, but I didn't know I was coming. The servants are following from the coast by boat, we raced ahead in Petronius's chair. He wanted to reach here before the wine ran out. Naturally we didn't manage it.'

The man smirked. 'You see, dear, Nero is in a snit.'

'*Fff!*' Julia Felix huffed a derisive breath. 'What about, this time?'

Caenis's chuckle was warm and pleasant. 'Petronius was less sincerely gushing than he should have been about the latest epic.'

' "The Burning of Troy", in I'll swear sixty million verses of – shall we say, unique – poetry, declaimed in that very – shall we say, extraordinary – tenor, accompanied by his beloved ivory lyre, over-gilded and under-tuned, slack in the higher notes, possibly out of sympathy with the voice. One felt ill. Well, under the circumstances, who could enthuse?'

'In spite of all the practice one has had!' Caenis sniped.

Pouting, he stuck the tip of his tongue out at her. 'Wicked!'

'It's the company I keep.'

'Too kind!' He acted shy, and lifted an eyebrow over a maliciously glinting eye. 'Better than boring!'

Julia Felix was chuckling; Victoria smothered a grin.

Caenis shook her head ruefully. 'So, Petronius decided it would be tactful to be absent for a while. He sent a letter excusing himself for his appalling lack of fervour on the grounds of illness, and begged our considerate Emperor's permission to retire to the country to recover. Which was granted—'

'With rather worrying alacrity, dear . . .'

'And he dragged me along as entertainment for the journey.'

'Well, one must have someone civil to talk to on the boat, or at least a competent nurse to cool one's fevered brow, or hold the basin in bad weather! One is ill, after all!' Hand to his brow, he pretended to be faint. 'And no-one, but no-one, is more civil and competent than Caenis. So, since Vespasian is off governing Africa – such an energetic, efficient person he is! – I knew Caenis was, shall we say *free*, dear. Not the right word, I know, but . . . So I rescued her from the throes of new frescoes.'

'And very grateful I was!' Caenis smiled.

He shuddered delicately. 'Painted plaster does stink so stinkily of cats! Not that one dislikes cats, of course. But one can have too much of even the best thing. The court is rabidly Egyptian this month, sacred cats under every tippy-toe; the cleaners are positively hysterical. I suppose one should be glad it's not sacred crocodiles. At least they keep down the rats. The four-legged ones, that is. The two-legged variety are in inexhaustible supply. Crocodiles might be useful after all.'

For an instant his expression was cynical and bleak before an impish grin again gave amazing charm to his mobile, ugly face. 'But now, Julia Felix, my everlasting loveliness, who, I ask again, who is this magnificent multi-coloured maiden whom we are ignoring so rudely?'

Julia Felix seemed embarrassed to be reminded of her earlier visitor. 'An acquaintance of my grandson. Victrix. A – er – a gladiatrix.'

'A gladiatrix? But—' Suddenly aware of Victoria in all her glory, Caenis was taken aback, as if she had slipped into a dirty puddle, but Victoria had to admire the speed with which the lady regained her poise. 'Greetings, Victrix. Is that your stage name – I mean, your name in the arena?'

'Darling, can you see any father calling his baby daughter "Victrix"?' Petronius demanded. 'But marvellously apt for a gladiatrix. If she's good – and I just know you are absolutely lethal, dear!'

'My given name is Victoria, Victoria Aegypta.' Victoria was agreeably surprised by their courtesy. The man had mentioned Vespasian . . . 'My father Rufius Aegyptus was a centurion in the Second Augusta Legion during the invasion of Britain.'

Caenis looked interested. 'Britain? Under Vespasian?'

'Yes, lady. He always said that Vespasian was the finest commander he knew – the only truly intelligent, honest and efficient officer in the army.'

As Caenis smiled in pleasure, Petronius sighed loudly. 'Well, isn't that nice! What a coincidence! What a small world! And all that boring nonsense!' He rolled his eyes in exaggerated distaste. 'Let us take it all as said, shall we? Victrix – such a challenging name! – Victrix, this lady is Antonia Caenis. *Best friend*, shall we say, of your papa's so-wonderful former officer.'

'Say *mistress* and tell the truth for once,' she told him, nodding amiably to Victoria and imitating her companion's waspish style. 'And this, shall we say *gentleman*, is Gaius

Petronius, called Petronius Arbiter. *Best friend*, shall we say, of Nero, Emperor of Rome, who has made him his judge of all things stylish and fashionable. Not knowing any better.'

'Darling, how perceptive! But only to think! Not clever to say, sweetie, even among friends. And we know nothing of this astoundingly ornamental Amazon. She could be reporting straight to Tigellinus.' He beamed at Victoria's bewilderment. 'Prefect of the Praetorian Guard, the only soldiers allowed inside Rome, dear, and, more important, head of the secret police. No, you've never heard of him, have you? Keep it that way, for your own sake, I do sincerely advise you, the man is a vicious Sicilian murderer. And no, that is not indiscreet, he knows my opinion of him, it amuses him.'

'He says!' Caenis interjected a warning.

Petronius raised a defensive hand. 'I know, I know! But in the meantime, Victrix, I'm positively enchanted to meet you! Are you staying to dinner?' He swung neat as a dancer back to his hostess. 'Darling Julia Felix, do say she is staying to dinner? I need her! I suspect that after all these years of official disapproval of bloodshed – what happens unofficially is of course unofficial – our beloved Nero is about to become enthused about gladiatorial combat. So I fear I must develop my knowledge of that, as well as of poetry and architecture, music and dress and astrology and all the arts. I'll soon be the world's only universal expert, everything from perfumes to plumbing! And here is a brand-new facet of the whole arena thing to intrigue our young master of the world, not the accepted view of the frowsty old philosophers and social moralists, but a perfect fountain of original and unexpected insights, straight from the Arethusan spring.' He winked at Victoria. 'And an extremely eye-catching nymph too!'

Julia Felix and Caenis exchanged a resigned glance. Victoria didn't know whether to be insulted or flattered. She was certainly interested and amused. She had never met anyone like him. And she didn't have to leave until midnight.

Besides, this Petronius was a friend of Nero. He could be useful. This might be the next step on her way to destroy Rome.

VI

Victoria did not pass on the story of how Pulcher had been mutilated. He had kept her secret about that embarrassing burst of weeping; she somehow could not tell his. Everyone in the palaestra accepted him now, but she knew them; if she told, he would face a new torment of secret sniggers. However sarcastic he was, she couldn't put him through it all again.

So at breakfast next day she described only the house and Julia Felix, the visitors, their clothes – which made Divina look very thoughtful – and every word they had said.

Her friends could tell her a good deal about the newcomers, in return.

'Antonia Caenis – yes, I know of her. She's a freedwoman,' Pulcher said.

Victoria blinked. 'She was a slave? Of someone called Antonia? Freed slaves take their former owner's name, don't they? But now she's—'

'The mistress of a senator, yes. An ex-consul, actually. She's been linked with Vespasian for twenty years. They met while she was young, a secretary to Antonia, mother of the Emperor Claudius. They just liked each other, I believe, and grew closer every year. Then one of the jewel merchants who sold to

Antonia fell in love with Caenis. Antonia freed her to marry him, but he died only a few years later. She's carried on the business herself, and very well too. Very expensive stuff.'

'Ah, that's why Petronius laughed when he said she wasn't free!'

'Why is this Caenis woman so popular, all pals with Nero's bosom buddy?' Africa asked, nudging Divina. 'We're always glad of tips!'

'Well, she's not exactly beautiful, but intelligent, incredibly stylish—' Victoria stopped at Pulcher's snort.

'In Rome there are hundreds of stylish women,' he informed her sourly, 'and intelligent ones too – unlike some places!' His eye was cold on them; Africa made a rude gesture that set them all laughing. 'But Caenis was one of clucky old Emperor Claudius's chicks. He knew her when she was his mother's young slave, and liked her – everybody likes her! So she was almost an imperial advisor. So everybody wanted to know her, to learn state secrets.' He paused, observing their envious faces. 'Sorry, girls, you can't compete there either. They were disappointed, though. Whatever bribes people gave her, gold, jewels, whatever, she stayed discreet.'

'Rare!' Divina commented.

He nodded. 'Indeed. When Vespasian returned from Britain, he and Caenis grew closer. His grandfather was a centurion who fought for Pompey against Julius Caesar, lucky to survive! Then he went in for moneylending and tax-gathering. They're not patricians, just country gentry, not even proper Romans, but Vespasian's father married a girl from a senatorial family, so her sons were eligible for the senate too. They're not poor, no banker is, but they could only afford to put their older boy, Sabinus, up the course of honour. Vespasian had to work for his advancement, with a good army reputation, and then pay his own way. Sheer determination and hard work. Mind you, he could never have done it without Caenis's help. She helped pay for games and so on, to get him elected right up to consul about ten years ago. Her friendship with Claudius didn't hurt him either.'

'He must be quite something, like my dad said, to persuade that lady to help so much! Did he not marry her?' Victoria asked.

'No, his father arranged a marriage for him. Vespasian's famous for doing his duty. Two boys and a girl. The younger son's still at school in Rome, but Titus, the elder, he's in the army in Britain just now, trying to calm the place down after your rabid queen's rebellion.'

'It's the Romans he needs to calm, from what I hear!' Victoria snapped.

His smile was twisted. 'That's what I mean. A reasonable, sensible young man, but tough, much like his father.'

Victoria snorted. 'At least one Roman family seems to have some decency!'

Divina was chuckling. 'How know all this, sir? Lady friends?'

He shrugged. 'They love to chatter, and it passes the time.' All three women exploded with laughter, while he looked smug. 'Caenis is well-liked, always pleasant and helpful. When Vespasian's wife died some years back, and Caenis was a widow, he wanted her to come and live with him, but she refused. He can't marry her, you see, it's illegal for senators to marry freedwomen, and I'm told she loves him too much to embarrass him. But the reason she gave – it made everybody laugh – was that he couldn't afford to keep her in the style she was used to. True enough. He's that rare thing, an upright man. His accounts send the treasury department reeling with shock, they're well-kept and not fiddled!'

'He'll never make anything of himself that way,' Africa commented.

Pulcher nodded. 'It's even taken him all this time to get sent out to govern a province, where anybody else would have got a plum post the very next year after being consul. As an honest man, and a provincial nobody, he has no influential patron or pull or friends at court except Caenis. I think she wangled him the governorship of Africa this year. It's a rich province, but he'll come back as poor as he went, you can bet on it. Maybe that's why she likes him, the difference between him and the rest. He's solid, sensible – sense of humour, yes, but not wicked. Unlike your pal Petronius, who is decadent, debauched, dissolute, disgraceful, dangerously – er . . .' He gave up trying to find the right word beginning with d. 'Attractive.'

Victoria nodded. 'He's all of that! Not handsome, but definitely fascinating.'

'And enormously extravagant. Arbiter of elegance, indeed! He only needs to lift an eyebrow at a tunic and Nero has the tailor flogged. He's writing a book, a satire on court life, and reads each chapter out at parties as he finishes it. I'm told it's very clever. The nobs all switch between screaming with laughter when they recognise their friends in it, and screaming with rage as they recognise themselves.'

'He certainly thinks he's witty,' Victoria agreed. 'And his manner!' She imitated Petronius's affected, hand-waving mince to make them laugh. 'You'd think he was crazy, till you see his eyes. They're colder than Glaevius's.'

'Well, no fool could have survived as Nero's closest friend for years. They say the Emperor takes his advice about everything. He's probably the most powerful man in Rome, after Tigellinus and Seneca.' Pulcher considered. 'No, more powerful than Seneca nowadays.'

'Seneca?' Victoria tensed at the name. Seneca's moneylending activities had had helped start the war in Britain.

Finishing a pear, Divina nodded. 'Nero's trainer.'

'Tutor,' Pulcher corrected her. 'He did his best to bring Nero up decently, and the boy did try to be a good Emperor for about five years. Not practical, mind you – he wanted to cut taxes, would you believe? But he got bored with piety and committee meetings, started looking for excitement, roaming the streets with his mates looking for mischief, mugging people and attacking girls. Good clean boyish fun. Seneca finally realised if he kept on trying to restrain his sweet young pupil, he'd be next to go. So he's retired. Wise man.'

Victoria had heard gossip about this, of course, but it was still incredible. 'The Emperor? Of Rome? Behaving like that?'

They laughed at her. 'Family tradition,' Pulcher announced airily. 'And compared to some of them, our young Son of God's a beginner. Of course, he's only twenty-five, he has time yet.'

Divina frowned. 'Son of God?'

Pulcher shrugged a bronzed shoulder. 'One of his titles. Every Emperor since the Divine Julius has been declared a god by his heir – apart from Caligula, who declared himself a god while he was still alive. So naturally Nero is the son of a god.'

'That's like something Manny was fussing over.' Lazily, Africa scratched the scar on her knee. 'You know that new Jewish sect, the scruffy ones who say bathing is wrong, and education and good clothes?' They stared at her. She shrugged. 'Their idea, not mine. I heard a couple arguing with the Jewish priests in the market while I was buying perfume. They don't approve of me, I can tell you! Anyway, Son of God, that's what they call their prophet. Joshua Crestus, some name like that. A sand-eater who went mad and claimed he was a god – and we all know only Caligula could do that! Caused riots in Jerusalem. Crucified for sedition, of course, before I was born, but they expect him to return to life any day and destroy the world – or maybe just Rome, and make them rulers of the world, I couldn't make it out. I don't think they know themselves.'

Destroy Rome? Victoria's ears pricked up. Could they be allies?

'Maggot-brained. But every second guy over there's a prophet or a terrorist, or both,' Pulcher sneered. 'They riot if the wind changes. The governor has to execute a score every year, at least. We've got two legions there to keep order, and it's barely enough.'

'Crazy,' Divina commented. 'Crazy people, crazy country. Lake there you can't sink in, just bounce on top! Crazy. But good fighters.'

'Not this lot, Manny says they're all slaves or freed, dimwits, losers and no-hopers, getting decent Jews a bad name.' Africa sniffed contemptuously. 'They'll never get anywhere. I don't know why he's so upset, worshipping a dead workman is no dafter than worshipping a god who isn't there, which is apparently what Jews do.'

'Mystic mumbo-jumbo and secret rites,' Pulcher snorted. 'The folk who worship Dionysus or exotic eastern gods get screaming drunk or drugged on mushrooms, so they have fantastic visions, and rip animals and children to pieces, or castrate themselves. *Yeugh*! And I hear this new Mithras is reborn at midwinter and washes his followers from their sins in the blood of a bull. Not my style.'

Africa grimaced. 'This Jewish sect holds suppers where they eat human flesh and drink blood.' Victoria kept quiet; the druids at home did that sometimes.

Pulcher shook his head in disgust. 'Give me a well-carved statue, respectable priests, regular prayers and sacrifices in return for agreed benefits, a straightforward business arrangement. That's civilised. If these grubby layabouts give their dead prophet one of Nero's titles, he won't be too happy.'

He became aware of the fighters round him gratefully relaxing, keeping quiet so that he'd go on chatting, and raised his voice. 'And if we don't get some work done for the games here in ten days, the boss is going to be fairly unhappy about that. He will make me very unhappy. And I will make you lot extremely unhappy. So, if you wouldn't mind moving your bulgy butts, you lazy slugs, we might possibly put on a show that wouldn't bore my old granny to tears.'

As everybody scrambled up, Victoria happily dismissed society gossip, politics and religion for the really important things in life. 'Petronius said he'd be coming.'

'Oh?' Pulcher sighed. 'Right. Better lay on something special for the Emperor's buddy. Get your gear and we'll work up a fight sequence to bounce them all off their fat little bums.'

Victoria whistled to the boy who dealt out the wooden weapons. 'Yes, sir. Who with? Divina's arm won't be healed by then. Tigris?'

'Me.'

'What? You?' He never fought any of the gladiatrixes. 'But – I don't want to kill you.' At his raised eyebrows and Divina's scornful chortle, she realised what she had said. 'I mean – I don't mean I'm better than you, sir—'

'I know what you meant,' he sneered, and then was suddenly angry. 'You're doing just what you've been warned against, time and again. I've told you, Divina has told you, everybody has told you – you must not get over-friendly! Kill or be killed, that's our job!'

Huffing, he seized a sword and shield from the lad. 'For Petronius Arbiter, we need something spectacular. But we'll try for a walk-off – skill, not slaughter, and everybody comes home happy. Well, as happy as possible with you around. Divina, get the girls fencing. Valerius, the retiarii's tridents are waggling like lambs' tails. Group one, boxing. Two, shield work. Three at the posts, four on the whirly, five on the heavy stones. Six, swing the clubs, I want to hear them whistle. Seven, wrestling. Eight, over the steps, hopping. Move! Right, come on, Victrix, and try to stay awake today.'

Fuming, Victoria moved out to the centre of the yard. She'd show him! He was as fast as she was, stronger in the wrist, and more experienced. But she could beat him, yes she could!

Why was he so harsh? He could sometimes be so different, so—

No. She refused to finish that thought, as she had done several times before, deliberately concentrating on professional matters. What would look good?

When Pulcher and Victrix entered the arena together ten days later, the crowd rose to cheer them. Her new gilded belt and parade helmet almost matched his in magnificence – she'd be able to afford armour and shield in time. Her scarlet ostrich plumes were as luxuriant as his. Her short scarlet top with its gold lacing, and red-and-black check trousers, balanced his crimson loincloth with the deep gold fringe. The women in the back rows – and several of the men – went crazy when Pulcher rippled his oil-gleaming muscles at them. All the men whistled at her.

Petronius waved a languid hand to return their salute, lounging in the centre of the magistrates' seats, surrounded by every one of the local nobs. Inside her helmet, Victoria grinned; yes, there was Ampliatus. Nobody would miss the chance to smarm up to Nero's friend!

As stars of the arena, she and Pulcher were put on as a single duel, not part of a multiple display, last before the final parade of survivors. Even in their plainer, practical fighting armour, they had bright cloth, crests and plumes – horsehair and feathers were cheap – and blazed like flames across the sand.

They moved all about the ring to give everyone a close-up view, ducking and weaving, their blades clashing metallic sharp over the screams of the crowd.

She was knocked down by a blow from his shield, to gasps from her fans, but recovered her feet with three fast back rolls and a flip. She'd pay for that later with bruises, but the effect was worth it. Later she drove him backwards till he fell; she courteously stood back, allowing him to leap up with his famous shoulder-jump. The crowd cheered both of them. Up and down they fenced, dancing right round the arena, working to very fine margins of error. He nicked her shoulder; she cut a shallow gouge down his thigh. A little blood could be spread a long, dramatic way.

Near the end, Pulcher skidded unintentionally and fell hard, leaving himself wide open.

The crowd would be furious if she just ignored the chance; they must know by now this was a rehearsed show, but they disliked being taken for fools.

She could have killed Pulcher, but snicked off one of his plumes instead. A roar of laughter rose when she snatched it up and stuck it into her own crest, clowning. As he jumped to his feet, he shook his sword at her in pretended rage. She strutted round, even turning her back on him – not rehearsed, but she trusted him to play along with her as she had done with him. The crowd screamed a warning. Deliberately slow in turning, she yelped; as she had expected, he had crept up behind her and smacked her bottom with the flat of his sword. Now it was her turn to shake her fist at him, before they swung into the final practised moves, fast and dangerous, that ended in a spectacular double cartwheel face to face. They broke from it, saluted each other panting, and turned to the crowd. Was it enough, or would the audience want a death? No; Petronius was standing, signalling for mercy.

No voice could have been heard in the tumult. Flowers, coins, purses, jewellery ripped from the necks and ears and arms of the audience, a rain of gifts poured down onto the sand. The arena slaves ran out grinning to gather it all up into baskets. As Pulcher and Victoria pulled off their helmets, the crowd erupted to their feet, shrieking the war-cry with Victoria, waving, dancing, fainting; their rival fans joined, for once, in a chant of 'Pulcher, Victrix! Pulcher, Victrix!' over and over, while they paraded round the arena to meet again in the centre, bowing and waving. Even Petronius was smiling and clapping.

They paraded five times round the ring together, laughing aloud in exultation. Pulcher caught her eye and for once smiled back at her in relaxed, open amity. 'Not bad, eh?' He was a great fighter, a great trainer – her hero, not just her trainer; an ideal man – she never noticed the scars now. He took her hand and raised it, generously proclaiming her equally champion with himself.

Suddenly her hand felt scalded. Her heart lurched. Her smile wavered, her breath caught short. She felt . . . she felt . . . so proud, so vulnerable, so – so shockingly much . . .

He saw it. His face changed. His smile vanished, to leave a blankness; then returned, artificial, denying her emotion, mocking himself and her. He dropped her hand, withdrew into his normal sarcasm. 'Wake up, you dozy savage! Wave to the nice people one last time before we go in and get fancied up for the final parade. Climb off your cloud of glory and pick up your feet. Back to the real world again.'

Obediently she followed him off. Her chest hurt as if she had a stitch in her heart.

On the way back to the palaestra he was withdrawn, accepting congratulations with an offhand nod and shrug, not joking or offering comfort, praise or criticism through the bars of the cart as he usually did. Inside the gates he vanished into the office and did not reappear.

She was relieved, even in her sudden insecurity. She had to think. She couldn't feel what she thought she felt. She couldn't! She mustn't! Not for a Roman. Not for anyone, till she had completed her task. And certainly not for him. He despised her – he made it plain.

When they were released from the cart she brushed past Divina and headed straight for her dormitory. To her dismay, the older woman came after her. 'What wrong, girl? You do good, we hear crowd from here. You live. Huge bag of gifts, and Pulcher always shares fair. What wrong?'

Africa had followed them. 'They both came off as if somebody had killed their kitten. And Pulcher isn't speaking to anyone.'

Victoria could no longer control her wretched misery. She slumped on her bed, nowadays the best one nearest the door, and pressed her hands over her face.

Exchanging a wry glance with Africa, Divina reached out a wiry arm to bar the doorway against the other girls. 'Go leave us in peace!'

As Victoria struggled not to wail aloud, her friends closed the door and sat down on the bed on either side of her. Africa put an arm round Victoria's shoulders. 'What is it? You can tell us.'

Divina sniffed. 'My guess, she wake up. See she love him.'

'No – no!' Victoria protested.

Divina merely grinned. 'We all know, girl. Even men! Everybody love trainer little bit, or hate maybe, but you love plenty, too plenty. We see. You watch him, feel him, know always, always where he stand. You try harder when he on palaestra. Is time you know.' She shrugged. 'I say you too warm, no good get tangle.'

Victoria snarled at her. 'Oh, everybody's warned me! Don't get friendly, don't get involved! But I didn't think I was, I didn't realise, not till that moment in the arena today, I didn't

96

know! Everybody but me knew, but I didn't! You've all been having a good laugh at me, I suppose, making a fool of myself over a man who despises me!'

'Despises you?' Africa's voice was astonished. 'Victrix, from the moment you swept off your wrap that first day, he's been goofy about you!' She and Divina laughed at Victoria's amazement. 'You're the only person who hasn't noticed it — we've been wondering if all Britons are as childish!'

'Oh, thanks!' She couldn't waste time and energy being annoyed. 'But — he's always so sarcastic, so cutting, harder on me than—'

'He's trying to keep you alive, girl! He's good at hiding his feelings, but it's been plain as the scars on his face!'

'Goofy.' Divina repeated the new word with relish. 'Yes. Eyes follow you. When you hit, he wince.'

'He's never said anything, nor acted lovingly.'

'Acted lovingly?' Africa laughed again. 'In here? Among these bawdy bastards? Neither of you would have a life worth living! Think, girl! He's the head trainer, he could order you to bed him, but he hasn't. When you first went out alone, he promised to go out to fetch you. He never offered that protection to us.'

Divina nodded agreement. 'You say you hit men try kiss you, he happy. An' drive, drive, drive, make you top top.'

'Divina's been green as a lettuce with jealousy!' Africa chuckled.

Yes, it must be true. All she knew about loving was Divina's and Africa's way, the kissing and coupling that she so often heard in the barracks, which had never attracted her. Pulcher had never even tried to kiss her, but he'd been kind and sympathetic when Victoria was upset – and never spoken of it.

Maybe that was a kind of love? Like the affection between her uncle and aunt in Britain?

Yes.

But equally, she had not told his story.

Could she really be – yes, admit it – *in love*? With a gladiator, despised by everyone? With a Roman? Could she . . . ?

Yes.

And could he feel it for her? Really?

Yes.

So why not tell her?

She looked at her friends. 'Does he think I'd be put off by his face? He must know me better than that!'

Africa shook her head. 'He doesn't want to distract you, maybe get you killed.'

Divina was nodding. 'Not want make you goofy too.'

'He isn't!' They chuckled at her leap to his defence, and she blushed all the way up under her tattoos. 'He's a fine man!'

They nodded, smiling. 'Goofy idiot,' Divina insisted.

Victoria sat back, rubbed her eyes and sniffed hard. 'So, what do I do? Catch him alone and speak out? Or wait, leave it to him, see what happens?'

'Speak!' Divina commanded decisively.

'Wait!' Africa recommended.

'A lot of help you are!' she scolded them, before hugging them. 'But you are, you are! But I suppose it's up to me to decide what to do.'

Even as they nodded agreement, she found her hands trembling and her stomach churning. She had never felt so nervous. Never. Not even when she faced the hippopotamus.

VII

The next morning Pulcher ignored her completely. For now, Victoria decided, she would say nothing either. That was one decision, at least; a definite postponement.

Just before noon, after an imperative banging on the outer gate, the guards on the walls jumped to startled attention. So did everyone else. The inner gate was flung wide for the first time in memory, and in strolled Petronius, leading a group of the leaders of Pompeii.

Victoria knew that every man of influence had a following of clients, as they were called, who were at his service in return for protection and favour, not just for money. Poor men might carry messages, gather in supportive, cheering crowds, or even beat up the patron's opponents; higher-class clients were companions or assistants; all would vote as the patron wanted in elections, on juries, in the senate. If the great Petronius, Friend of the Emperor, Arbiter of Elegance, took a whim to visit a smelly, vulgar palaestra, then these nobles of Pompeii – patricians and equestrians, senators and magistrates, men who would normally no more have entered a palaestra than bathed in a sewer – were delighted to accompany him as temporary clients.

'Don't stop, don't stop your training! Ah, there she is! Victrix!' Petronius minced forward, gilded fingernails flashing, his mocking eyes inviting her to play along with his exaggerated foppishness. 'My dear, what an utterly stimulating performance yesterday!' His companions chorused eager agreement. 'And here you are now among your deliciously muscular comrades! Nero must see you, he really must! I'll take you back to Rome with me. Our beloved Emperor will be thrilled to meet such a colourful character.' He quirked an eyebrow at Victoria's scalp.

Rome! Victoria's breath caught. Exactly what she needed to fulfil her geas! Oh, wonderful! But . . . 'I'm bound to the school here, sir.'

Petronius smirked, infuriatingly superior, and waved a casual hand. 'Gladius here will lend you to me!' Flushed, but as always expressionless, Glaevius nodded; no-one argued with the Emperor's friend. Petronius beamed at Victoria. 'You see? No problem, my warlike wench! So you will come to Rome with me, and dazzle the court with your deadly derring-do and your scintillating skin!'

If she went, she would lose Pulcher.

Did she have him?

She never would, not if she left.

Her face lost its delight. 'I can't, sir! I – I really can't!'

The Pompeiians gasped in horror. Even Glaevius blinked. Petronius's mobile eyebrow shot up. His eyes were suddenly hard. 'Reluctance, sweetie? Most unwise. What you really can't do is refuse.'

From the rear of the group, Pulcher stepped forward. 'Lord, may I speak? Under her confident surface, Victrix is shy.' Several men nodded, and two chuckled. 'Allow me to accompany her to Rome, to advise her how to behave, and continue her training so that she can do herself and Emperor Nero proper justice by putting on shows such as the one which you enjoyed.'

Glaevius's rigid face turned furiously purple at losing both his stars.

Victoria's heart beat so hard she felt it shake the world like an army marching. Pulcher was finally looking at her, smiling slightly, ruefully, lovingly. Her insides were melting. He cared enough to leave his secure niche here, go out among the wounding curiosity of strangers, to help her. She swallowed. 'With Pulcher's support, my lord, I am – I'm happy and – and privileged to come.'

The mobile eyebrow flickered again. 'Such a relief! Though a gentle gladiatrix seems a perfect paradox!' As the hangers-on applauded his wit, Petronius rolled a wicked eye at Victoria. 'So delightful, to find one's predicaments so happily resolved! Now, show me round, darlings, do, and explain every little detail!' He fluttered like a butterfly towards the whirly, his entourage scurrying after him.

As they moved round the palaestra, from one group to the next, demonstrating and describing the training, Victoria could scarcely bring her mind to concentrate on what she was doing or saying. Pulcher was coming with her, away on their own, away from the bawdy gossip and joking of the palaestra. She was walking a handspan above the gravel. Her chest felt stuffed with feathers. She touched Pulcher's arm as if by accident. Her hand fizzed and sparkled. He did not turn to look at her, but from the side she could see his lips quirk briefly.

The gate opened. A Praetorian, red cloak flaring, red crest bristling across his glittering helmet, marched across the palaestra, scattering the nobles as if they were hens in a farmyard. Saluting Petronius, he presented a scroll. 'From the Emperor Nero, to Petronius Arbiter!'

Petronius looked delighted. 'Ah, the dear boy hasn't forgotten me! Thank you, centurion. His Imperial Majesty is in good health? Excellent! And good voice? Ah, splendid! Such incredible talent . . . Excuse me, gentlemen.'

While he read, his followers exchanged excited, nervous glances. Was Nero inquiring after his health? Announcing a gift? Requesting advice? Commanding him to commit suicide?

'His Imperial Highness summons me to his villa at Baiae. Joy! Centurion, you are riding? Yes, I can smell the horse. Be a darling, gallop down to the harbour. A galley that can set me and maybe twenty others ashore at Baiae within one hour gains ten silver sesterces for every oarsman.' Petronius's lips twitched. 'You'll have to fight off volunteers.'

A slave had appeared at his master's shoulder. Petronius spoke without looking at him. 'My personal staff will be ready to leave ten minutes after I reach Julia Felix's, and if Antonia Caenis wants to come with me so must she be.' As the man whirled away, Petronius beamed at his companions. 'Gentlemen, I do regret, but when the Emperor calls one does not run, one flies.'

Smiling sweetly at their murmurs of disappointment and awe, already moving towards the exit, he snapped his fingers to Victoria. 'Victrix, my tender turtle-dove, with me. And your – er – your manager.'

'What? Now? But—my armour, my clothes . . .' Behind her, Divina and Africa shot off one way, Glaevius's slave boy and Pulcher another.

Petronius paused momentarily to regard Victoria in astonishment. 'My charming cherub, you can buy new, or what's-his-name can send them after you. You come. Now.'

In the passageway four big matched fair-haired Germans in Petronius's peacock-blue uniforms knelt by the poles of a gilded carrying chair. Four other servants were already helping the porter open the outside gate. Victoria dropped a pinch of incense into the lamp flame as she passed: 'Thank you, Bouda. I think.'

Divina handed her a bag: 'Clothes!' Africa had a smaller: 'Your purse and jewellery!' She hugged them heartily, until Glaevius's boy shoved a clinking sack at her: 'Your good gear,

104

Miss Victrix, an' your sword!' He bobbed a bow. 'Good luck, miss – do us proud!' Behind them, crowding round the palaestra gate, jostling the affronted magistrates and even the guards, the other fighters were cheering.

Petronius rolled his eyes as he settled among the silk cushions of his chair. 'What it is to be popular! Someone carry her things. To Julia Felix's, fast.' Men seized Victoria's bags – she clung to the one with her precious torc – and the well-trained bearers raced the chair smoothly up the road.

Victoria was breathless, and not just from the rush of keeping up with the chair. Once again, her life had been turned upside down with no warning.

Pulcher pushed into the group of servants running beside her, and grinned at her. 'Thought you'd lost me?'

She grinned back, suddenly filled with energy and enthusiasm. But she couldn't think what to say. 'Thank you,' she finally managed.

'I always wanted to see the world.'

This light, sardonic tone she could handle. 'You're not coming just to hold my hand, then?'

'Me? You? Never. I wondered if I could make Glaevius change expression.'

'Fat chance of that!' She laughed, breathlessly, and bit her lip. 'But you hate going out – and you've given up so much—'

'Nothing that won't be waiting for me – for us – if we want to come back.' He lifted a finger. 'No buts. I'm coming because

I want to. Because I was afraid for you, in Nero's court. Because I didn't want to lose you. Nothing that I've given up is worth more than you are.'

With sheer joy her heart expanded so much it was hard to breathe, let alone speak. 'That – yes, I felt the same. That was why I tried to refuse.'

He glanced at the servants round them. 'We'll find a time to talk, alone. Soon.'

At Julia Felix's house, Petronius vanished indoors. A bustle of peacock tunics was already loading two mule-carts by the door. Six more bearers fell in behind the chair. 'How many slaves did the man bring?' Victoria wondered.

'Well, he was visiting a friend with a fully-staffed house. Only thirty, maybe.' Pulcher chuckled at her gape. 'Yes, really. He'll have three or four hundred at his home in Rome, plus others to look after each of his country villas, maybe a thousand in all. Some men with huge farms to run have as many as twenty thousand!'

Julia Felix followed Petronius out, and then Caenis, a maid adjusting a dust-veil over her mistress's hair. Petronius kissed the old lady's painted cheek: 'You angel, angel, not to scold me! Duty calls!'

'Nero calls!' Caenis snipped, stepping into the wide chair. Four of the spare bearers joined their mates at the poles, to carry the extra weight.

'Same thing, my honey-sweet! Ready?' Petronius sank into the cushions again. 'Wine, Melanippus? Under the seat? Excellent. Melanippus, my toga-draper and Caenis's maids in the carts. Victrix and my other staff for the palace come behind. The rest will follow as swiftly as possible.' He gazed round expectantly. 'Are we waiting for something?'

Victoria trotted among the spare bearers and running slaves, feeling Pulcher's arm brushing hers. 'More interesting than dodging round the palaestra!' he commented over the rattle of the mule-carts cantering behind.

Nodding, smiling, she settled to enjoy the run down to the sea, through the vineyards and olive groves. It was good to be out, away from the school, away from the town; from the in-turned, greedy curiosity of the palaestra; from the coarse, callous jesting that disguised the eternal tension. She felt almost free again. And with him . . . Yes, Pulcher loved her, and yes, she loved him . . . Life was wonderful!

Caenis glanced over her shoulder at Victoria's flushed, exalted face, and eyed Petronius thoughtfully. 'You – we need to speak to her.'

He nodded. 'I know. You, my fragrant flower, are expert in the ways of the court. But our newcomer . . .'

'Yes. Naiveté can be attractive, but ignorance is dangerous. She could easily, unintentionally, get you into serious trouble. And herself, of course.'

'Exactly, my perfect peach. But your support and advice

will make her believe my words of warning. As soon as we're away from ear-filled corners.'

At the harbour the centurion was waiting with a sleek thirty-oar skiff, its oars poised ready to fall and bite the water. He saluted Petronius. 'Fastest available, sir. Double oarsmen. Captain swears he'll have you over the bay before you can blink.'

'How excellently efficient!' As his steward slipped the soldier a discreet purse, Petronius whisked Caenis up the gangplank. The servants were scurrying to carry the luggage aboard. As soon as Petronius set foot on deck, the captain yelled, 'Let her go!'

'Come on, dozy!' Pulcher yelled urgently. The gangplank toppled into the water as the ship was shoved off from the wharf. Victoria had to leap to grab the bulwark, one foot actually sousing into a wave. Pulcher helped her over, shaking his head in amused reproof. 'You'd miss your own funeral! Look, your posh pal's beckoning.'

Floating on happiness, she moved reluctantly from his warm arm round her shoulders towards the stern, where Melanippus, unruffled from his jolting in a mule-cart, was serving wine to Petronius and Caenis under a small awning. 'Yes, sir?'

Petronius glanced round, a carefully casual inspection. The oars, bending under the full thrust of professional rowers determined to win their bonus, were banging and creaking in their holes. A boy was beating a drum to keep the rowers in time. The rush of wind and waves created a lot of noise. The captain at the tiller nearby was unlikely to overhear. 'A little advice, my vivacious very-nearly-late Victrix. On how to handle our sublime ruler, Nero, First Magistrate, Emperor of Rome. Because this, my perilous pet, is an arena you are not trained for.'

'He's a young man of twenty-five, Victrix,' Caenis said, 'with an appalling upbringing and no check whatever on his actions. He has the Empire's wealth to play with—'

'Not as much as he had, dear,' Petronius put in. 'Even a bottomless well has limits!'

'And you're helping him find them.' Caenis's voice was caustic.

'Tossing money at playwrights and sculptors keeps his claws – I mean, keeps him happy. While he has Tigellinus and the pampered Praetorians to protect him, he can do anything, Victrix. Absolutely anything. You know the family history?'

Victoria hesitated. Better not mention the gossip. 'Something about adopted sons?'

'Indeed.' Petronius's mouth was wry. 'No Emperor has been succeeded by his own son. The real heirs have all been – whisper it – murdered.' Victoria drew a deep breath. He nodded, smiling bitter-sweet. 'A little history lesson – but not dull, I promise you. After Julius Caesar was murdered, his nephew and adopted son Octavius Augustus became the first Emperor – and had Caesar's son by Cleopatra killed. Augustus married a beautiful lady with a young son, Livia, given the title Mother of the Country, gods preserve the country. Year by year, all Augustus's own sons, grandsons, sons-in-law and nephews were found guilty of plotting against him, exiled and executed – apart from those who simply died. So tragic! And pure coincidence that one Lucusta, known to be a poisoner, was a great friend of Livia, and in and around the palace regularly . . . When Augustus had no heirs left, Livia persuaded him to adopt her son Tiberius. Then Augustus died. Not unexpected – except by him . . . And Tiberius became Emperor. His hobbies were extremely – shall we say, *unusual.*'

'And just as well. He liked little boys. And girls. Say *vicious* and *disgusting*,' Caenis commented dryly. 'Tell the truth!'

'Truth, my petal? How bizarre! Not that I disagree . . . When he was old, Tiberius fell ill, but looked as if he was recovering till one of his former childish playmates, his nephew and adopted son, Caligula, smothered him to take over the throne. So impetuous! As a child, Caligula had already murdered his father. Now he executed one sister and exiled a second – Agrippina, our beloved Nero's mother, sent off to a desert island leaving her unfortunate toddler to be reared by Caligula's slaves. Then he declared he was a god and married his third sister – yes, truly – and when she was pregnant, killed her and ate their unborn baby. Don't look sick, sweetheart,

110

that's what gods do, look at Saturn. This was our present Emperor's childhood home.'

He smiled sourly at her dropped jaw. 'When the Praetorians killed Caligula – a squabble about promotion or pay, I believe, not civic principles, they have none – they crowned his elderly uncle Claudius next, more as a joke than anything else. His mother was the lady Antonia, Caenis's former mistress, and he was her last remaining son. All the rest had – *died*, shall we say? Only poor old Claudius was left.'

'Claudius wasn't bad,' Caenis commented.

His eyebrows rose. 'Only in comparison, dear. He used to have people tortured as dinner entertainment.'

'He did his best,' Caenis insisted.

'Ah, well, you knew him well, you should know . . . His third wife – or fourth, was she? – Messalina was fourteen when they married, and he was about fifty. She had several senators murdered before she married her lover Silius – the latest of dozens, I assure you, Claudius was blindly besotted with her, the old fool – intending to divorce and kill him – Claudius, not Silius, of course, don't be silly – and rule through their young son Britannicus. Beautiful, but a totally incompetent planner. Even Claudius couldn't turn a blind eye to that. He executed her, and to fill the gap in his life married his niece Agrippina, the only sister Caligula hadn't killed.'

'*Aargh!*' Caenis growled. 'We warned him about her. But he

felt sorry for her and her pretty little Nero, who was a delightfully charming child – he'd had to be, to survive, of course. And Agrippina acted amiable, but she had a will of iron underneath.'

'Barely underneath, my precious. Claudius's son Britannicus should have inherited the throne, but when the old idiot married Agrippina, he adopted Nero, who was a year or two older than Britannicus, and married the lad to his young daughter Octavia. Perhaps he was worried that Britannicus would turn out like his mother Messalina, and wanted an alternative choice. Mistake! Agrippina poisoned Claudius to make Nero Emperor while Britannicus was still too young to rule, and then they poisoned Britannicus, too, two days before he reached adulthood at fourteen and could argue about it. He was a conceited young ass, but had a better singing voice than Nero, which obviously encouraged our golden boy to dispose of him.

'Then Agrippina claimed she had made Nero Emperor: true. And started bossing him about in public: tactless. She even had her head stamped on the coins beside his. Then he wanted to marry a slave girl, Acte. Illegal, of course, quite impossible, but Agrippina was the one he blamed for forbidding it. So he had her killed. Yes, his own mother. Do close your mouth, plum, you'll catch flies. He tried to poison Agrippina, but she sicked it up. So he sent her home on a ship specially built for arena combats, to fall apart when the captain pulled the lever . . . But to his vast peeve she managed to swim ashore. He had to send soldiers to stab her with their swords – terribly upsetting!'

Petronius smirked at Victoria's awed face. 'Not bored yet, dear? Then Nero fancied Poppaea from Pompeii. He ordered her to divorce her husband, who might argue, and marry Otho, one of his friends, who wouldn't. But then he fell in love with her and wanted to marry her properly. So he told Otho to divorce her and sent him off to rule the richest province in the Empire as a reward, while Nero first tried to strangle his present wife, the terrifyingly virtuous Octavia, then divorced her, and then had her executed.' He shrugged extravagantly. 'A terribly wasteful hobby, murder. Every word true, isn't it, Caenis?'

'It's all the most vicious gossip, of course, but I suppose . . . Yes.'

'Yes.' Petronius nodded. 'Nowadays Nero's friend, the Praetorian Prefect Tigellinus, keeps accusing people of treason. Rich people, naturally, and irrefutable evidence – the best informers rewards can buy. Brings in millions, for no trouble! You see, the Emperor gets all a traitor's possessions. But if the accused kills himself before trial, he can save half – everybody has to leave Nero half their money in their wills – and our golden boy doesn't get the bad publicity and nuisance of trials.'

Yes; the King of the Iceni had left Nero half his money, and

Caenis was nodding again. Victoria decided it must be true. 'Why does he need all the money?'

'He's desperate to be loved, would you believe?' Petronius's voice was acid.

'It's true.' Caenis chuckled sadly. 'He gives out thousands of presents – clothes, money, jewels, horses, ships and city blocks and farms. He builds extravagant palaces. And he's an artist.' Petronius cleared his throat. She flashed him a quick smile. 'He thinks he's an artist. But it's hard on any man, let alone an all-powerful Emperor, to long to be a genius, but to know deep down, where he can never admit it to himself, that he isn't. So he encourages the arts. He organised a great theatrical festival to celebrate the glorious eternity of the Empire. One senator rode an elephant down a tightrope.'

'So inspiring! Don't you feel inspired, petal?'

'He's set up the Neronia,' Caenis went on. 'Like the Olympic Games, but for plays and music, games, poetry, horsemanship, gymnastics. Nobody would object to that, and he gives amazing prizes. But he competes, himself. As a religious ceremony it doesn't quite count as a public performance, which would horrify everybody, but the conservatives are still shocked.'

'Shocked? When they first heard him, they were aghast.' Petronius's supple fingers framed his face like petals round a sunflower. 'But who'd dare mark him down? He wins every prize for oratory, verse-singing and lyre-playing.'

'He tried to abolish gladiators, didn't he?' Victoria asked.

'And nearly caused a revolt,' Petronius sneered. 'As long as the grain supply stays regular and cheap, and the Emperor only kills off nobles, the mob quite enjoy the scandals. It's all good gossip. They even attend his boring Neronia – it's free, and he gives out food and little gifts to the audience. But watering down their blood sports they didn't find funny. They even objected when he tried to make fights stop at first blood. So Poppaea, who looks as brainy as an orchid but is actually nobody's fool, is persuading him to take an interest in the games.' He lifted a finger. 'And that, my amazing Amazon, is why you are here.'

Victoria tried to look intelligent. 'To show him what it's really like.'

'Exactly wrong, my sweet swordmistress.' Petronius and Caenis exchanged glances. 'You see, he loathes bloodshed. Odd, you think? But there it is. It thrills and fascinates him, but also revolts him. So you must show him the glitter, the skill, the daring – but not the horrid bloody stinky facts.'

'You have a fine line to walk, Victrix.' Caenis was sombre. 'If you toady to Nero too much, he's not stupid, he'll see it, despise you, and make you fight every day till you're killed. If you're too brash – and especially if you ever hit him, Julia Felix told me about Ampliatus—'

'Hit him? Hit . . . ? Oh, Jupiter!' Petronius shrieked in exaggerated horror.

'Oh, stop that!' Caenis cast him a vexed glance. 'Even look as if you might hit Nero, Victrix, and you'll be executed. You must keep him enthralled, keen to hear and see more of your fighting, but not too greedily excited, or you may tip him into open blood-lust, when he'll kill you just for the thrill of it.'

Victoria grinned. 'I can do that, lady. I've been playing the crowd and the dinner parties. There's more to being a top fighter than just being good with a sword.'

Again, the others exchanged glances. Caenis shrugged. 'Better confident than trembling. But Victrix, please be wary. You're a straightforward person. The court is not. Nobody there is your friend. Nobody. Whatever anyone says, everyone you will meet is not merely indifferent, but eager to drag down anyone who threatens to exceed them or their patrons in Nero's favour. Trust no-one.'

Petronius giggled. 'That includes me. Doesn't it, my candid Caenis?' As she nodded he pouted, not insulted, stuck out the tip of his tongue, and winked at Victoria.

She had to smile, even as Caenis warned her, 'He jokes about everything, but this is serious. If you told Tigellinus what he's been saying, well, it's the word of a gladiatrix against that of the Emperor's friend, and mine, which has considerable weight, and I'd have to back him to keep my own life safe. I hope if Petronius sees Nero growing tired of you he'll send you away, back to Pompeii—'

Petronius looked hurt but forgiving. 'Of course!'

116

'I said I hoped so. But . . .' She glared at him, before returning her level gaze to Victoria. 'But given the choice between your wellbeing, your life, and any threat to his own, or even to his own comfort, then goodbye, Victrix. Remember it. Trust nobody.'

'Yes, lady.' Victoria hugged to herself the knowledge that Caenis was wrong; there was indeed someone she could trust. With her life.

VIII

The journey across the bay took less than an hour. Victoria stood at Pulcher's side, watching the silver ripples gusting across the dark-blue water. They could not speak, not among the crowd of slaves and spare rowers, but their hands touched on the rail and time melted away . . .

A year later, a moment later, the ship bumped the quay below the sprawling marble palace on the hillside. Briskly, Petronius whisked them all off into a reception suite. 'Your finest dinner party wear. Half an hour.' He and Caenis vanished.

A slave dropped Victoria and Pulcher's bags inside a doorway, and swept out. 'Well, I suppose we can slum it for once,' Pulcher commented loudly to the man's disdainful back.

'Don't be daft!' Victoria grinned. 'Look – our own private pool!'

Pulcher did not reply. She turned, and found him taking her in his arms.

'I've wanted to do this since the moment I saw you, so tall and proud and bright, hiding your fear with audacity . . . I tried to tell myself you were a barbarian, but you weren't. You fought so fiercely, but you insisted on being friendly; you were kindly and generous and clever . . . And if your head is savage, so is my face – no, it's true, but it didn't matter to you! With you I feel at ease. Oh, my dearest dear . . .'

She almost sobbed in happiness at last.

At length, reluctantly, Pulcher sighed, grinned, slapped her bottom and shoved himself away. 'Come on, into the pool, mustn't keep the Emperor waiting!'

'What huge sponges! Rose oil, lavender and – what's this? Sandalwood, that's for me. Turn round and I'll scrape your back . . . Stop tickling! Look, ivory combs.' They smiled constantly, like mischievous children, and their hands tended to linger.

They were just ready in time, smelling exotic.

Petronius inspected them, nodding approval of Victoria's wolf-skin jerkin, her brilliant Iceni shirt and trousers, and Pulcher's not-too-short blue tunic with the silver belt, while three servants unrolled a long segment of a circle of snowy, polished linen, three arm-spans long and one deep in the centre, with the senatorial wide purple stripe round the curved edge. Two kept it off the mosaic floor while, quarter-turn by quarter-turn, the expert draped the toga round Petronius over his green-and-gold gown, arranging the folds with exquisite precision. A final inspection, a gentle adjustment, a dab of chalk powder on a barely-visible mark, and the man nodded reluctantly. 'It will do, sir.'

Petronius sighed in theatrical relief as the servants left. 'I'm a martyr to that man's quest for perfection, I assure you,

119

darlings. One fault and he'd have stripped it off me and started again. He carries two spares, in case of accidents.'

Victoria was intrigued. 'Is that all he does for you, sir? Arranges your toga?'

'The arbiter of elegance can scarcely look scruffy! Talking of which, leave your headscarf off; Nero must get the full flavour—Ah, here's Caenis. A vision of loveliness!'

'You need an eyeglass.' Irritably arranging a bracelet, Caenis sounded testy. 'For an important occasion, I need two hours at least. My eyeliner—'

'No, no, my perfect peach, you look delightful, and the gewgaws will have all the women positively slavering! Not to mention the men!' He twinkled at her. 'Besides, with our flamboyant warrior maid and our heroic – er – hero, not to mention my humble self, who's going to be looking at you?' She snarled at him, and they laughed together.

This villa was a new level of wealth again for Victoria; a hundred times bigger than Julia Felix's, more sumptuous than the richest banker's house. As they strolled along frescoed corridors and marble colonnades, glimpsing through windows and archways manicured gardens and other buildings all around, she found her mouth dry and her stomach unruly. Aware of her tension, Pulcher touched her hand. She almost forgot her anxiety in the delightful rush of tingles.

Everyone they met stared at Victoria and Pulcher, then ignored them while saluting Petronius with respect. Caenis, elegant as any in her white gown and gold-and-jet jewellery, smiled serenely; to some of the richly-dressed courtiers Petronius lifted a gracious hand or nodded regally or roguishly, bowed to none, once paused to embrace a young woman and – even more extravagantly – her handsome companion.

As they approached a gold-beaded curtain veiling an outside archway a sweet-faced girl hurried up to them. Petronius paused. Murmured words: 'But I did send . . .' After a moment Petronius smiled genially and they moved on, while the girl bit her lip and scurried off again.

His face was bright and assured; his mutter was furious. 'Leave him alone for ten minutes and this is what happens. A public performance, would you believe? Singing in a theatre, like a paid entertainer. He'll offend the whole senate, every patrician in the Empire. As if I hadn't told him . . .' He hissed in disgust. 'At least he's doing it in Neapolitanum, not Rome. It's an old Greek settlement, and he thinks they'll appreciate his singing more. Knowing Greeks, he could be right.'

Caenis was frowning. 'And someone stopped Acte's message to you? Tigellinus?'

'Probably. And no-one has mentioned it to me. That is more worrying than—' Noticing Victoria and Pulcher, he beamed kindly. 'But not excessively, my angels! His Imperial Highness is on the terrace. Wait here till I call you.' Smiling, he pranced out into the sunlight.

Outside, Victoria had been vaguely aware of someone practising scales. The voice was light, breathy, and straining on the higher notes. It stopped.

'Oh, no, sire! Please continue! Such delicate breath control!'

A slim, ringed finger parted the strings of gold nuggets to let Caenis watch, paying tense attention. All the men and women behind them, Victoria realised, were inching close like vultures.

'Ah, Gaius Petronius! My dear, how are you? Quite recovered, I hope?'

Caenis drew a deep breath. 'He's still in favour.' Her shoulders slackened a touch, in relief. 'Now, when you're called, go out, kneel, call him "Caesar", or "sire", or "Your Imperial Highness". Good luck!'

'Will you not be with us, Antonia Caenis?' Victoria asked.

Caenis chuckled, a warm, friendly sound, surprising among all the glistening marble and the intent watchers. 'Me? A freedwoman, a trader? No, dear. I'll stroll around, remind everybody that I move in good company, flash the gems, chat, probably be invited to dinner. They're all frantically curious about you – can't you feel it?' She nodded encouragement. 'You'll do very well, I know, but if you need help come to me. Ah, he's beckoning. On you go!'

'Bags of swank!' Pulcher muttered. Victoria just glimpsed Caenis's surprised blink before his hand on her shoulder urged her through the tinkling beads, out onto the terrace, and down to her knees.

By the marble balustrade, just beyond Petronius, stood a young man – tall for a Roman, plumpish, with a thick neck below lush golden curls and a wispy golden beard grown to conceal terrible spots and a double chin. He was tugging petulantly at the gold-braided neck of his royal purple tunic. 'I knew it was baggy, but that fool insisted . . . I'll have his hands cut off.'

By chance he moved slightly aside so that Petronius's bulky toga hid Victoria from him, and he saw only Pulcher. Instantly, he stiffened and flung round away from them, a hand over his eyes, his voice rising in horror. 'Oh, no! No, really! Ugh! How could you, Petronius! You know how deformity upsets me! How dare you bring such a hideous sight before me? Revolting!'

Stiff-faced, Pulcher was about to rise, but Petronius gestured to him to stay where he was. 'Sire, who knows better than I how sensitive you are? For ten years you have honoured me with your friendship. Would I wound you without excellent reason?' Soothing, like a nanny with a fractious child, Petronius drew the Emperor further away, his hands waving as he talked.

'Pig! Rotten stinking callous pig!' Victoria hissed, flushed in fury. 'And his lousy arbiter of elegance too!'

Though tight-jawed, Pulcher could smile to her. 'Don't fret,

I've heard worse,' he whispered. 'But thanks.' His appreciative look warmed her.

'Pulcher!' Petronius called, lifting a finger. Pulcher rose and walked forward to kneel again beside Nero, who gazed unseeingly out over the sea, his shoulders hunched in distaste.

Victoria clenched her fists. If he was so spiteful again, she'd – she'd . . .

She'd go on kneeling here and seething. He was the Emperor. He could do anything he liked. Have them arrested, exiled, executed – anything. Oh, Bouda curse Petronius for bringing them here!

Now Nero peered down towards Pulcher, tentatively, face half averted. His hands hovered over Pulcher's face, the fingers writhing together as if they were sticky, and then ventured forward to actually touch the horrible scars. Delicate, tentative at first, the fingers flinched away, then stroked and poked more confidently in fascination. Pulcher knelt still, the tendons in his neck standing out like cords at the humiliation, but his face expressionless. What else could he do?

Petronius glanced back and shook his head at Victoria in warning.

No! She had to do something. But what? She couldn't just kick the big purple pimple right off the balcony . . .

She coughed.

Tutting at the interruption, Nero glanced round and for the first time saw Victoria kneeling there, her tattoos glowing in the sunlight. 'What . . . ? Who . . . ?' He recoiled, and suddenly stiffened. His jaw dropped. Abandoning Pulcher, he waved urgently for Victoria to rise, twiddled his hand for her to turn round and be inspected on all sides. 'Oh, Isis! Can it be . . . ? It isn't possible . . . Oh, Isis!'

Behind him, Petronius's blank face camouflaged his perturbation.

'Come, come!' Nero seized Victoria's wrist and dragged her through the curtain, along corridors and through hallways, past alarmed servants who dodged away round corners, past guards who snapped to rigid attention, drawing behind them a scurrying tail of Petronius, Pulcher and the courtiers from the inner hall like a hen followed by a clutch of agitated chickens, through a gilded doorway into a fine, big, airy room with a balcony looking out over the sea; his bedroom.

Dropping her hand, he rushed to the bed.

Purple silk sheets, Victoria noticed. Why bring her here? Surely not . . . ?

No. He tossed his piled silken pillows carelessly to the floor to reveal an ornate gold box. Clutching it to his chest, panting in some overpowering emotion, he turned to face her, and only then seemed to become aware of the jostle in the doorway. 'Out, out!' he screamed. 'No, not you, girl! You stay!'

Reluctantly, Pulcher followed the courtiers out, peeking round the door jamb.

Petronius stood still. 'Should I leave also, sire?'

'*Um . . .*' Nero studied him, and then shook his head till his plump cheeks wobbled. 'No, stay. You –' He held up the box. 'You don't know what this is. Not even you.'

'No, sire.' Petronius's voice was soothing. 'Clearly an object of great importance to you.'

'Yes.' The Emperor laughed, a high nervous whinny. 'Importance. Yes.' Drawing a deep breath, he forced himself to speak more calmly. 'Two years ago, Acte gave me this. She said it was from the daughter of a friend, who was ill. The child said the goddess Isis had told her in a dream to give me her most precious possession, which would protect me. It had protected her for years, but now it must be passed on to me. So Acte gave it to me – no, I said that – and the child died that same night. Isis's protection lost, you see? But before I knew that, I didn't know, you see? I thought it was a child's fancy. But Acte, sweet girl, she believed. She hid it in my pillows. And that same night, I was warned about a plot to kill me! And then I found it, and I knew it was true. What the girl said, you see? A true vision. Yes. I've kept it ever since. All the gods are . . . I never believed, not after Caligula – but this is different. I've never told anyone. And this is it. Look now. Look! You see?'

Reverently he lifted from the box a simple ivory statuette the length of his hand.

'Scythian, possibly—' Petronius started, and then halted and stared at Victoria.

The doll was dressed exactly like her – trousers, tunic and jerkin.

'Look, even the head, I thought it was curls, but . . .' The head was marked with tight curves, like Victoria's tattoos. 'And here, you see?' On the figurine's back was carved a tiny wolf's head.

Under the wolf's head of her jerkin Victoria's shoulders crawled, while her lost hair tried to stand on end.

'You see? You see! She protects me, and now she's here in the flesh! It's magic! It's fate! A gladiatrix, you said, didn't you? She's sent by Isis to guard me, protect me like the figure.'

'Oh, sire!' Petronius raised his hands in surrender to obvious awe.

Nero was almost weeping. 'I'll keep you with me, girl, forever! You're a miracle! Always at my side. People hate me, madmen, plotting – but you'll keep me safe! You'll eat from my plate, and sleep in here, by my bed. Not more than ten paces away. Never!'

What an amazing, perfect position! But when would she see Pulcher?

Victoria knelt, to please the Emperor, and as he paused for breath, she interrupted gently, ignoring a frown from Petronius. 'Great Caesar, you honour me too much. I do truly believe the gods have sent me to you. But with respect, I can't stay beside you every minute.'

'Why not?' Nero was puzzled, more than angry. 'Why not?'

'Sire, my presence would embarrass you. Your nobles see gladiators as low ruffians—'

Petronius snorted amused scorn. 'The Emperor of the world should care what anyone else thinks?'

'But more than that, Highness, I'm a fighter, not a fancy girl. I need to train for hours every day, to stay fit and ready to protect you.'

Nero looked bewildered. Petronius hummed pensively. 'She does have a point, sire. A fat and flabby fighter – oh, we can't have that!' He shook his head. 'Naturally she must remain in the peak of condition. I wonder, sire, might I make a suggestion? You might consider instructing the girl – Victrix – to exercise only while you are safe. Perhaps while you are rehearsing. One can scarcely expect a girl from the wilds of Britain to appreciate your musical genius.'

Nero was nodding thoughtfully. 'True. True.'

Victoria, however, huffed aloud in annoyance. Petronius tutted at her. 'Now, now, my violent violet. It is not polite to interrupt the conversation of one's superiors.' He smiled condescendingly to Nero. 'A simple country maiden, sire—'

'I admit, sir, I am unused to courts,' Victoria stated crisply. 'I say openly what I think.'

'How refreshing!' Petronius chirruped. A lifted eyebrow and a cold stare warned her not to go too far.

'But I do indeed appreciate music. In Britain, a bard is more revered than a king. Kings are born; a matter of luck. But even a person gifted by the gods needs twenty years to train as a bard, learning the great songs, studying the arts and skills of singing, playing the harp, making new songs. Among us, if a bard makes any request of a king, it must be fulfilled, to the last drop of gold or blood in the kingdom!'

Nero saw himself as a great musician; surely this must please him? Yes! He almost glowed with delight. 'How wonderful! You must tell me all about these – bards, did you call them? – of Britain. Perhaps I shall go there to meet them!'

You've killed off most of them, she thought in sudden resentment.

'Go? To Britain?' Petronius shuddered. 'Oh, dear! So cold and wet!'

Dreamily, Nero waved that aside as unimportant. He'd be protected from the weather, anyway. 'Music is a universal language. Soul speaking to soul, your bards and I! You open new horizons to me, Vic – er, Victrix? Yes, Victrix. I was not aware the savages in Britain were civilised enough to have any culture at all!'

Thank you, Victoria thought snippily, but kept her face calm. She was becoming as much of a crawler as Petronius! Well, perhaps not.

'Oh, I am so glad I found you! Gaius Gratidianus, Aemilia Plautia, see what I've discovered!' Nero swept off, calling in excitement to his courtiers.

Petronius's eyebrow was twitching as he ushered Victoria

after the Emperor. 'More sides than a starfish, my multi-talented marvel.'

Pulcher's tension relaxed visibly at the sight of her, safe and well. Petronius smiled. 'A teeny hint about your – *friend*, shall we say? Our beloved Nero likes to be first in everyone's heart.' His murmur became flirtatious. 'You do realise, though, that your unexpected enthusiasm for music was a grave mistake, my rose with many thorns? It has brought you a grim misfortune – one might almost say, *tragedy*!'

She eyed him with misgiving. 'Tragedy, sir?'

He laughed, drawing her forward as Nero beckoned. 'When Nero gives any performances from now on, you are going to have to attend!'

IX

Empress Poppaea, bright, chirpy, astonishingly beautiful, and charmingly bossy, was so aristocratic she need not consider Victoria's infamous rank. 'I'm really looking forward to seeing you fight, Victrix, I've heard so much about you!' She chattered amiably to this disgustingly low-class female as if she had not a thought about anything except pleasure. Maybe she hadn't; or maybe she was simply a good actress, as Petronius thought. Victoria had a great respect for his astute judgement.

However, Poppaea was the only one who readily accepted Victoria.

Disgusted that the Emperor's new favourite was a gladiatrix, the stiffer patricians ignored her as they would a dog. She ignored them right back.

Many of the younger clients had heard of her from friends in Pompeii; she had to dish out several well-judged bruises before they acknowledged that she was not available, not even to palace patricians.

The status-sensitive palace slaves and freedmen who actually ran the palace and the Empire were mortally offended by this scum suddenly high among them. Instantly, of a single mind, they determined to be ostentatiously

131

polite, while actually plotting every possible annoyance and offence.

However, while Victoria was on duty Pulcher was free to wander among the stables and passages, chatting. His patrician birth, tragic mutilation and downfall gave everybody a satisfyingly superior shiver. As a result, he made friends. When he told people Victoria would rather be in the arena than here, they tended to believe him rather than sneer cynically. After only two days, before she had even realised the full depth of their initial hostility, the servants and officials began to accept her, treat her as a person, discover that she was in fact not too appalling after all; even fairly pleasant.

Every morning she rose from a pallet beside Nero's bed when Acte brought in the perfume that he offered to his little idol three times a day. Everybody liked sweet, soft Acte, who was always helpful, and not very bright, with her huge dark eyes constantly alarmed. She loved Nero unselfishly, arranged flowers and made sweets for him, scented his pillows, knitted his socks, worried about him. The only woman in Nero's life, Petronius said, who never tried to order him about.

When Acte left, valets entered. While Nero was being dressed, his poison-taster took a mouthful of each of the twenty dishes offered for breakfast, from honeyed wheat porridge – much better than the palaestra stuff, as Victoria, eating after the Emperor, found with relish – to poached peacock eggs.

One day Victoria tried out the old joke: 'Caesar, why is a

peahen cleverer than a peacock?' Nero stared in bewilderment. 'Because a peahen can lay peacock's eggs, but a peacock can't lay peahen's eggs!'

'Impertinence!' He slapped her, and giggled as her face froze. 'You must never make fun of your Emperor!' Then he smiled, that charming smile that he used so consciously, and tapped the fingermarks on her cheek with an admonitory finger. 'Naughty girl! But since it's you, I'll forgive you!'

Later that day she heard him asking a senator, 'Why is a peahen cleverer than a peacock?' and crowing with delight when the man tactfully did not know, and all the toadies applauded. Really, the man was so childish! In some ways. Not in all.

It didn't seem to occur to him that she might find it less easy to forgive him. Or that his smile might be less beguiling in a man of twenty-five than it had been in a lad of ten.

No, that wasn't right. He actually relished the certainty that whatever he did, he must be forgiven. To show offence was treason. Let all his boils burst at once!

Every morning he went swimming with his friends, his hair carefully tied in a hairnet to preserve the curls; or hunting, with deer being driven in front of a shooting stand or basketfuls of hand-reared birds freed around him as he strolled along the wooded paths of the estate with his bow, and only a dozen guards and servants to hold his arrows, towels, socks and spare sandals, a snack, wine, comb, an ivory folding chair and cushions

133

in case he was tired . . . Victoria had to be very close to him then; 'A stray arrow – so easy, an apparent accident, you see? Be on your guard!'

If he felt energetic he might go riding, or chariot driving. Roman horses were much larger than Iceni ponies, and trained differently; Victoria found she could not handle them. To her mixed annoyance and pleasure – anything that gratified him made her more secure – Nero guffawed, and delighted in showing her how it should be done. He boasted about having driven in races in the Circus Maximus in Rome: 'All the senators were horrified – silly old fogeys! I've driven two and four horses – you've never driven four? It's far harder! And four camels, too! Nobody else has ever driven four camels!'

Who else would want to, she wondered. But when, on a generous whim, Nero offered, 'Will I teach you to drive?' she accepted gladly. Though he lost interest after only five sessions, while it lasted she learned a great deal, and it gave him – and her – an honest satisfaction.

His government advisors claimed him for a while before his first hour of vocal exercises, which he took far more seriously. He sometimes spoke to them lying on his back with weights on his chest, to strengthen his breathing. During this time Victoria could go off with Pulcher for training and practice.

To her acute annoyance, whether they went to the back courtyards, the stables, the banqueting halls, the gardens, they could never find any privacy. An audience of skiving slaves or curious courtiers seemed to grow from the marble. 'I'm trying to get a room to myself,' Pulcher assured her. 'But it's unheard of, for a man of my low status. I'm lucky to have a bed in a room with only ten others.'

Even when they did manage to evade their spectators, to her frustration he would do no more than kiss her. 'Not now, not here. When we have time to enjoy it. When we're free.'

Victoria tutted at him. 'You sound like Divina: "Get tangled, lose sharp, lose life!" '

He hugged her. 'And she's right – especially here! Remember Petronius's warning. I'll not risk Nero hearing gossip about us.'

She pretended to hit him. 'Coward!'

But he was right; even as he laughed and fended her off, a slave appeared round the corner, calling, 'Here they are! Victrix, what are you practising today?'

Picking up her wooden sword, under her breath she growled, 'Patience!'

Even like this, though, it was joy to Victoria, to be so close at last to her love.

After Nero's noon snack and his second sacrifice to his little figurine, he took a siesta before two more hours of singing. Again, Victoria could use this period to train.

Then it was time for him to be formally dressed, have his hair re-styled and his face painted for dinner. Victoria, hoping

135

her stomach didn't rumble, stood behind his couch, ready to leap forward if any servant or guest snatched out a knife. She could lift a surreptitious meal from the rejected dishes, far beyond those of Popidius's feast. She found she disliked peacock's tongue pies, the vast muddy-flavoured cat-fish of the Tiber, and honey-coated monkey brains, and preferred the simpler things: braised leeks, roast chicken, sardines fresh fried. Everything was tepid at best; the kitchens were too far away for anything to come hot to the table, and then Nero's tasters had to check every dish for poison.

After the evening entertainment – singers or dancers, jugglers and acrobats, philosophical debate, dancing dogs, Nero's own music, or drinking and gambling – he often bet four thousand silver sesterces on each pip of the winning throw at dice – she retired to her uncomfortably soft, fleecy pallet on the floor by his bed.

Every few nights she was called on to give a display fight. The first time, Pulcher was waiting in a side room with their gilded parade armour. She was puzzled, for she knew Glaevius had sent on their plain fighting armour. 'Why the fancy gear?'

He flicked one of the high-relief figures with a scornful finger. 'More impressive. We'd better wear it, even if it's not so practical, Vicky.' She grinned, warmed as always when he called her by her pet name. 'Lift your arms till I fasten you up. We'll do a simple version of the arena fight. You still remember it?' He chuckled as she sneered. 'That's my girl! But miss out your back flips, there's no space; after the high cuts we'll go straight to my attack on your right flank. We'll get showy another day, involve the slaves, slash cushions to send feathers flying, go up on the couches over the guests—'

'Wow, that'll be a riot! Even your old granny would enjoy that! Don't you dare smack me, I'm the Emperor's pet! But seriously, tonight, who wins? Or do we make it a draw?'

'Not the first show. Nero would never let you die, Vicky, but if I beat you first time he could be annoyed and next time you win, deny me mercy in sheer pique.'

'I'd never kill you, Pulcher. I − ' the word still made her stammer shyly − 'I love you. I couldn't.'

He gripped her shoulders. 'I love you, too. That's why I'm saying this! I'm serious. Fortuna keep it from us − but think, girl! I'll not allow death by torture for you. And I hope you'll not for me.'

'I'd kill Nero first!'

'Quiet!' He checked that no-one had come in, and then grinned. 'Thank you. But don't be daft, the Praetorians would mince you. So this time, you'll win. After my attack, you drive me back, I'll let my sword fly. With any luck it'll hit a senator. Here's Petronius − sir, if Victrix wins two fights in four, I win one, and one's a draw, that should be about right? We want both of us to survive.'

Petronius's gilded fingernails flashed as he clapped his hands in affected joy. 'Ah, bliss that at least one of you can think! Not that you can't, my fabulous female fighter, but you're – now how can I say this?'

'Without getting your teeth knocked out, sir? Simple-minded?'

'Say – *unwise*. And de-toothing me, so to speak, would be proof of it. You're clever as a multitude of monkeys, I know, but wisdom and cleverness are not always found together. Simple-minded is not how I would ever put it, my sweet!'

She laughed, holding down the fizzing excitement and fiery nervousness in her belly. 'How would you put it? Or where?'

'Ooh! Naughty, already?' He tutted at her. 'Pulcher, my muscular model of masculinity, you really must keep your delightful doxy under control! Now, are you ready? Our golden boy is agog with anticipation. Couldn't be agogger. Not a pretty sight.' He coughed. '*What* a pretty sight, I meant, of course. I simply adore your feathers – such a pity they wouldn't go with a toga! Could I start a new fashion? No, perhaps not even I could . . . Come along, then.'

'Right, Victrix!' Pulcher recalled her to formality. 'Helmets on, heads up, bags of swank! We're on!'

From the moment they marched in to raise their swords together to the central couch and shout the traditional salute, 'Hail, Caesar! We who are about to die salute you!' they were a wild success.

Up and down the room they fought as they had done in

the arena, while Nero and his guests, and even the slaves round the edges, gasped, shrieked and cheered the flashing, clashing blades.

Most of the guests were senators and philosophers, here to show how cultured and trustworthy the Emperor was. These were – or at least pretended to be – primly shocked. However, there were several younger nobles, Nero's wild pals of nights out on the town, interested in the raffish pleasures of the stage, race-track or arena, like Victoria's hosts in Pompeii. They whistled, yelled in delight: 'Give it to him! That was close! Nearly got him that time! Stick it in!' and ruder comments. Poppaea, on Nero's right on the top couch, was one of the noisiest.

Victoria enjoyed both reactions when she could spare the time to think of anything except the fight, for Pulcher seemed bent on killing her. His blade drew a horrified squeak from Nero when it sliced her leather top, producing a fat trickle of blood down her belly; she realised she was fighting shy, speeded up and managed to swipe off another of his feathers before they came to the final flurry. When Pulcher let her knock his sword from his hand, he was careful that it flew up in a dangerous-looking arc but into an open space – where by good luck it stuck upright in a melon on a bowl of fruit, looking very dramatic. Then he knelt, gracefully bowing his head as he raised a hand. Above him, Victoria did the same.

Nero waved to Pulcher to rise, gasping in excitement, 'Oh, Jupiter! Yes, yes, of course—*Aagh*!' Victoria, as was her custom, had snatched off her helmet and screeched her war-cry. Even she was startled at the din that echoed round the marble halls. Nero nearly fell off his couch. 'What – what's that? Oh, Jupiter Optimus Maximus! Oh, oh, what a show!'

Gradually he calmed himself, and raised a hand to still the applause. 'Your Emperor is pleased to be pleased!'

Pulcher nudged Victoria. Of course; here she was the leader. Lay it on thick; 'The Emperor's pleasure is our only aim!'

Still palpitating with excitement, Nero beamed. 'I bestow on you the title of Imperial Gladiatrix!' He beckoned. She stepped forward – and halted as the Praetorians jumped forward. 'No blade near the Emperor!' their officer shouted.

'Don't be silly! How can she defend me if she's unarmed?' Nero flapped an irritated hand at them. 'Now, Victrix, sit down here and tell me all about your career.' A stool was instantly placed beside him. While the soldiers drew back, offended, Pulcher slipped out, not removing his helmet.

Nero and his wife questioned Victoria eagerly, showing less foolishness, on the whole, than some of the self-styled experts in Pompeii. 'Are you never afraid?' the Emperor asked.

'During a fight you're too busy. Before it – every time, sire.'

Poppaea clapped her hands in astonishment. 'I was sure you would boast, "Only cowards feel fear!" or "Never!" '

Victoria did her best to imitate Pulcher's raised, sardonic eyebrow. 'Anyone who never feels fear is a numbskull, lady. It's only when you are afraid that you can be courageous.' They all applauded.

One of the philosophers asked, 'How many people have you murdered?'

'None.'

'Oh, come, don't play the innocent!' The man smoothed his beard condescendingly. 'You could not become so famous without having killed dozens!'

Insulting, arrogant pig! Don't snap at him, or crawl; deny the enemy what he wants. Control, politeness, posh speech, good sense so that he can't sneer – and hit back when you can. 'Several, sir. But I do not do murder.'

He sneered anyway. 'And how do you distinguish between murder and what you . . . er, do?'

'Murderers kill illegally, privately, for personal benefit or pleasure. I kill openly, as allowed or demanded by the law. Rome's law, that you made, not me. In the arena I'm the hand of Rome, as much as any Praetorian.' She gestured at the stone-faced Praetorians on offended guard round the room. 'I only kill people facing me weapon in hand, trying to kill me, or condemned to execution, or else, in the arena, if the crowd calls for death. I kill only those who Rome decides are due to die.'

There was a brief silence. Then Nero asked, eyes bright,

'How does it feel? I mean, when your blade slides in? How do you feel?' He licked his lips.

This question often arose at dinner parties, always with this same greedy, contemptuous fascination. As always, she answered factually. 'In the heat of a fight – satisfaction in a true blow. An execution or a mercy killing – disgust, pity sometimes. But I have to do it, so I do. Afterwards – pleasure that I've won, relief that I've survived, sorrow, nausea, always. But . . .' she shrugged. 'It's part of the job. You have a drink and put it away.'

'You don't enjoy the blood, the feeling of power, the act of killing? Or feel guilty about it?' Nero tried to seem merely casually curious.

'No, sire.' She met his snigger with a straight glare. 'Yes, I'm a volunteer, I chose to go into the arena. But it's the fighting I enjoy, the thrill and excitement of the risk, the applause and the chance of glory, not the killing. Some do, I grant you, but the people who get pleasure from the blood are the audience, not the gladiators.' She looked round; some faces were surprised, some thoughtful.

'Everyone, everything, dies sometime – of miserable old age if nothing else. I'd rather die swiftly in the arena. Clean and quick. It is cruelty that is evil. Hurting and destroying for position or pride, greed or fun, and enjoying the pain. And it's the crowd who do that, not me.'

The audience was silent, taken aback by her lively defence of her profession. From Nero's left, Petronius, his face mocking, came to their rescue. 'Incredibly articulate! One would scarcely have expected such deep philosophy from a common gladiator! Or are you an uncommon gladiator?'

'You know little about gladiators, sir,' Victoria challenged him, setting his eyebrows bouncing. 'Yes, the palaestra is rough, it doesn't encourage delicate sensitivity, but there are intelligent people there, as outside. And some of us do discuss what we do. More thoughtfully than you obviously believe.'

A senator huffed. 'Rubbish! Vicious murderous brutes, criminals, mutinous slaves, violent trouble-makers, enemies of Rome!'

She could have taken Needle and stitched the old fool to his puffy cushions, but she didn't. Control . . . And with the Emperor's patronage, despite being socially so far beneath them all, she could say at least some of what she felt. 'Thank you.' She had the satisfaction of seeing him blink, realising that he had been describing her, too. 'Many are brutes, yes, but not all. And think, senator. If you break a man's arm, do you blame him for wearing a splint? If you brutalise a man, who is responsible for his brutality?'

Her breath caught; a great deal of what she had said about the evil of wanton killing and cruelty could apply to Nero himself. Was he offended? Or had she upset Petronius by telling too much of the truth? No, they were both smiling, applauding her – though in a patronising way that showed they didn't care about a word she said, as if a donkey complained that it disliked pulling a cart. Annoying, but safer that way. Thank Bouda!

Next day, when Victoria spoke to Pulcher about it, he just nodded. 'Nero thinks he's so superior that ordinary opinions and law simply don't apply to him. All criminals do.' He grimaced, and shrugged. 'Forget him, back to business. Your footwork was sloppy last night. I've scattered our armour and weapons and a few stools and rocks round the yard here. Race you fifty times round each way, forwards and backwards.'

As usual, a dozen slaves were lining up to run beside them. Oh, well, it would make a better crowd for dodging. 'Ready? Go!'

X

'So what was it like?' Pulcher asked. 'Bad?'

'Diabolical.' For once they were alone, if not secluded, sitting in a quiet corner by one of the pools in the villa gardens on the evening of Nero's great concert while courtiers strolled and gossiped nearby. 'Petronius exaggerates about Nero's singing, but not much. And his poetry – *yuk*! "Sing, sing, ye bee-full glades, ye buzzing orchards, sing, sing the beauty of the sacred spring! Sing, sing, ye trees, ye flowers and ye bowers, sing, sing the Muses' song of everything!" ' Victoria rolled her eyes.

'He was sick before he went on stage, with terrible stage fright. But once we shoved him on, the audience were well primed, they all cheered and begged for more over and over. He didn't stop till he could barely whisper. Six whole hours, with just a few breaks while a choir sang more of his songs. There was a little earthquake, but he was so lost in his music he didn't even notice it! Nobody was allowed to leave, either. I had to stand at the side of the stage the whole flaming time. The Praetorians are used to sentry duty for hours, but I'm not. Gods, my feet and back were killing me! At least I could sit down on the boat coming back; he was flat on his back with doctors dripping soothing oils down his throat. Soaring on clouds of triumph, but he can't speak a word.'

'Poor dear!' he mocked her.

She regarded him suspiciously. 'Which?'

'His Imperial Majesty, of course!' He winced exaggeratedly at her playful punch on his arm. 'Ouch! Big bully! Me, I took a very pleasant sail back to Pompeii.'

She perked up. 'How is everybody?'

'They all sent their best wishes. Divina got a bad stab last week.' He tapped just below his left collarbone. 'She finished her opponent, but she'll be off for at least a month.' His eyes lifted past her. 'Duty calls! Here's Acte coming.' He grimaced ruefully. 'Like a soft-boiled egg, my old granny would say.'

Laughing – Acte wouldn't know why – Victoria smiled up at the huge, rather vacant eyes. 'Does the Emperor want me, Acte?'

'Yes, Victrix, the Emperor wants you.'

Victoria chuckled; thinking up her own words was always hard for Acte. 'Why?' No, unkind. Suggest something, to prompt her. 'Are we going to Rome?'

Acte had to stop, nervously poised for retreat, and ponder. 'No – yes – no ... Two more concerts. Then we'll go. To Rome. Yes.' She looked pleased with herself for having answered fully.

'Oh, well. There are worse places to hang about. The armourer has to alter my new greaves, the buckles are too low.

I don't think he realised just how tall I am compared to you titchy Romans. But why is Nero calling me now?'

Acte had had time to think. 'The sculptor Artemidorus wants you to model for him, for a statue of an Amazon. Nero wants to see you in different poses.'

'Fame! And cramp! Oh, well. See you later – my love.' At her murmured endearment Pulcher shook his head and tutted. Yes, he was right; she must not say things like that, even under her breath. But she wished he was less – less honourable. Hurried kisses and cuddles in a corner, always wary of intruders – he could surely find somewhere private, even for an hour, if he really tried!

Victoria used Pulcher's strong shoulder to support herself to her feet, caressing his neck as if by accident, enjoying the twitch of his muscles under her fingers, and spoke more clearly to any snooping ears – curse them all! 'We could be on again tomorrow. So don't just sit there and doze, dozy, plan some new fights.' His lips twitched; his hand rose to touch her fingers.

A month later, the court left for Rome. A flotilla of seventeen galleys followed the Emperor's own ship, providing all the comforts of home. Three carried a selection of courtiers. Two held guards; two, Nero's and Poppaea's clothes; others were crammed with the cooks, the main kitchen and supplies for the three-day voyage, the musicians and secretaries, Nero's chariot and horses and their attendants, the rest of his baggage and the lesser servants.

The only time Victoria had sailed before for more than a short boat trip was in a small, grubby cargo ship bucketing across the Narrow Sea from Britain. This was very different.

The imperial trireme had a sail of purple linen, walls painted with scenes of romantic islands, and bronze braziers in which incense and sweet-smelling apple charcoal warded off any chilly sea breezes that penetrated the heavy silk curtains. Its crew wore smart purple-bordered tunics, and when necessary rowed to the music of a small orchestra, not a common drum. The opulent dining couches were lemon-wood, carved with tritons, upholstered with softest golden suede. Nero's bed was fully as big as the one in Baiae, with embroidered curtains and scented cushions.

One cabin held a marble bath with warm, scented water. While Nero drowsed dopily in it, Victoria was free to wander round, talk to the sailors, wave across to Pulcher on one of the servants' ships.

The second day, as she swung from a rope, her face alight with mischief, gibbering and scratching her armpits like a pet monkey, neither of them noticed Nero come stretching out of a doorway below her.

He blinked up at her, peered to see who she was play-acting for, and frowned.

'Caesar! A snack, sire?' Petronius called. Distracted, Nero

148

rejoined his friend and Poppaea. But the jealous little memory lingered.

On her walk to Pompeii, Victoria had already admired the huge gilded temple of Jupiter Optimus Maximus on top of the Capitol hill, towering above the Forum Romanum; the dozens of marble statues and smaller temples, some only a single dingy room, squeezed among the mansions and apartment blocks; the wide marble colonnades, market halls and squares; the royal palaces shouldering each other up the Palatine Hill; the vast Circus Maximus racetrack; the multinational crowds that jostled through the narrow, smelly lanes shadowy under rickety ten-storey tenements in the Subura slums. She had made an offering in the Pantheon Temple, dedicated to all gods, for success . . . Marching now through the cheering streets behind the Emperor's chariot, she wondered how she had dared. To pray to Rome's gods for help in destroying Rome was surely remarkably silly.

Once again she was astonished by a new level of luxury. Nero's palace, the Domus Transitoria, was smaller than his country villa, but far richer. 'Why Transitoria?' she asked Pulcher. 'That means a passageway, but it doesn't really cross from anywhere to anywhere.'

He shrugged. 'Maybe it's just a temporary palace, passing the time till he can think up something really special.' They laughed together; what could possibly be more special than the crowds of statues, the frescoes and mosaics, the gilded ebony and ivory furniture, the shelves of scrolls in the library – unread, but there – the agate and glass, silken drapes and embroidered cushions?

However, Empress Poppaea was less than happy. She disliked Rome's gawping crowds, the constant noise, the confined, close buildings, and especially the stink. Even the vast drains under the city could not remove all the stench of so many people, and perfumes and incense only compounded the reek.

To make things worse, she discovered she was pregnant again.

Overjoyed, Nero set himself to please his wife. What would keep her occupied and content? Jewels? Clothes? Music? Flowers?

'Games, sire?' Petronius suggested. 'Lots of lovely lions, the finest gladiators, a delightful little picnic, strawberries, chilled wine?'

'Oh, yes!' As always, Nero picked up the idea as if it was his own. 'We'll have special games of celebration. Who can we dedicate them to? The immortal Julius, founder of the line? And we'll have the local stars fight Victrix! A treat for all of us!' He beamed graciously at Victoria.

In the first two games, Victoria killed both her opponents. Local men, neither had the skill and panache that Glaevius and Pulcher taught their gladiators. They did a workmanlike job, though not good enough to win, nor to cooperate with

Victoria as Pulcher did and put on a display leading to a draw. For the first time, Nero saw her fight to the death.

The day after the second games, Petronius paused in a corridor to smile sweetly to Victoria. 'You remember what Caenis said? About our golden boy getting a taste for blood?' Victoria nodded. 'He has been terribly enthusiastic about the games, and the hunts, and the other fights, and especially about your wins, my perilous peach. A touch, shall we say – *over-enthusiastic*. Avid, even. You might try to – er – tone down the gore?' He produced a cascade of melodious laughter, flirting gilded fingernails, acting casual to the always-present audience. 'I can't think exactly how – dreadful to have to admit ignorance! But it would be wise.'

'I'll see what we can do,' she said thoughtfully.

Pulcher visited Maximus, Victoria's opponent for the third fight, to suggest a display fight, but came back disappointed. 'He's insulted at being hired to fight a gladiatrix, even for ten thousand sesterces prize. If crazy women want to be slavered over in the ring, they should stick to the comedy shows, he says.' Victoria sniffed scornfully. Pulcher continued, 'You'd think he'd have realised that you can beat any man alive – except me, of course. Don't you dare hit me, I'm your manager! No, he'll fight seriously, Vicky. And I hear he's good. Fights as a provocator, with a small breastplate. You might have trouble with him. Don't be over-confident and try to be too fancy!'

'I'll take care.' She was carefully oiling her arm-plates,

ensuring they would slide easily. 'This will help, it's excellent.' The new set of armour Nero had given her was a perfect fit and, since Pulcher had spoken severely to the armourer, engraved rather than embossed, smooth enough to be practical despite the gold inlays. 'I'm not going to get killed before I'm free – before we're free! But I'll put on the best show I can to keep Poppaea happy. The poor woman's feeling all swollen and ugly, Acte says, and constantly sick. Pleased about the baby, yes. And glad that Nero is pleased too. But she had a miscarriage last year, and she's terrified it will happen again.'

Pulcher nodded thoughtfully. 'No wonder. Nero adored his little daughter who died. What'll he do if Poppaea loses this baby, or it dies too? Console his wife, or blame her?'

'She's all chirpy and smiling as usual,' Victoria said, 'but underneath . . . Acte says in private she's easily upset and bad-tempered.' She bit her lip. 'In a way, she reminds me of Atalanta, determinedly cheerful.' Not a happy thought.

Now, when they were due to set out, Poppaea sighed, 'Nero, my dear, I'm really too tired. No, don't fuss, sweetheart sire, I'll be fine! You go on, have a good time, and come back and tell me all about it!'

Maybe better relaxed without her, Nero seemed to enjoy himself even more. He had tokens for prizes tossed into the audience by slingers, and giggled as the crowd fought for the tokens. He laughed even harder at the thought of some of the prizes they were killing each other for; not just a sack – or a warehouse – full of corn, or the winner's weight in costly pepper, but a box full of fleas, or a pair of old socks.

In the final match, when Victoria won again, her right hip pouring blood after a hard-fought, scrambling combat, the audience reaction was mixed. Many cheered the new champion, and joined in her war-cry as the crowd had done in Pompeii; however, several booed, unhappy that this incomer, and a woman at that, had killed their own local hero.

The Emperor was rather peeved. People had no business not supporting his protégé! While Victoria paraded round, limping, Nero spoke to Petronius, and then beckoned Victoria to stand in front of the royal box while the heralds' trumpets sounded for silence.

'Victrix, Imperial Gladiatrix!' Nero announced. 'In admiration of your tremendous skill, we present you with the Villa Glauca and its estate!' At last everybody cheered. He beamed with pleasure.

Armour was magnificent enough, but a villa! Had any gladiator ever been so richly rewarded? Victoria hurried off to get her wound stitched up, wash and change, and find out about her new property.

As always, Pulcher had already made enquiries for her. 'It's not far off, about three miles, by the Anio River. Not big, but good, nice vineyard. Its owner was accused of treason last year, killed himself, and this villa was part of what he left to the

Emperor. Hurry up with that towel, get back and thank him properly!'

She did so, so thoroughly that Nero almost glowed with gratification. Partly because he felt so virtuous, he did not hurry home, but stayed out drinking and gambling with friends, including Petronius, who was always careful never to be too big a winner.

They returned to the Domus Transitoria after midnight. Acte was waiting for them at Nero's bedroom door. 'The Empress Poppaea has been asking for you, sire.'

Hand to his head, he grimaced. 'No, it's too late.'

But, 'Oh, please, sire!' Acte murmured gently. 'She missed you.'

'Ah, poor woman! You always bring out the best in me, Acte! I'll tell her about the games.' Comfortably benevolent, he lurched down the corridor.

Victoria waited outside Poppaea's bedroom. Rather to their surprise the Empress's maids were sent out too, and took the chance to flirt with the Praetorians on guard duty. Victoria leaned against the wall beside Acte, easing her bandages, chuckling at the whispered chit-chat – until rising voices inside the room froze them.

Complaints and scolding growing louder, more insistent, shriller; angry retorts and argument; a slap; Nero's screech of outrage; blows, screaming – a shriek, 'Help! Help!'

Victoria led the rush to the door.

Poppaea was curled on the floor, wailing while Nero kicked her, stamped on her, yelled incoherently. 'How dare you? You can't – you mustn't! Stupid insolent – cow! Traitor! I'll get you! I'm Emperor – Caesar! How dare – you worm!'

Victoria didn't know what to do. Hit him? Drag him away? As she hesitated, Acte ran forward and seized Nero's arm. He hit out at her in a blind fury, but when she cried out he realized who it was and stopped. 'Come–come away, master! Over here – sit down, now,' she murmured soothingly.

The horrified maids clustered round their mistress, lifting her gently back to her bed, carefully ignoring Nero. Poppaea was moaning in pain.

Nero collapsed onto an ivory chair, watching them, his mouth open, panting, distressed. He clutched Acte's arm. 'I, I need – Poppaea, you – oh, Isis! – she shouldn't – she was – I'm the Emperor – I—' He gulped, and vomited noisily and messily. Snivelling, he used Acte's shoulder to heave himself to his feet and lurched past them to the door.

Acte pattered after, to support him. Aghast, Victoria barked at the girls, 'Send for a doctor!'

'I am a doctor!' one snapped back.

'Will she be all right?'

The woman glared, saw Victoria's sincere concern and shook her head doubtfully. 'I hope so.'

There was nothing Victoria could do here to help Poppaea. She went to help – not Nero, but Acte.

Nero shivered violently as they staggered along the hallways, but was blankly withdrawn by the time they reached his room. He sat in a trance on the edge of the bed while in terrified silence his valets stripped and washed him. By the time they rolled him under his silken sheets he was already snoring.

Poppaea died before dawn.

It was announced that she had had a miscarriage, and died. Next day, she was cremated in a hurried ceremony, scant of music, offerings and mourners. Nero did not attend. Poppaea's family was represented only by an ancient uncle, the man who could be most easily spared if Nero decided to strike at his wife's friends . . .

Even Petronius was subdued. He paused three days later beside Victoria, who was exercising with Pulcher below the terrace where Nero was chanting mournful bits from his 'Burning of Troy' epic. 'Have you noticed, sir,' she asked quietly, 'how good a lie you can tell by simply not telling all the truth? Everybody knows, of course, but nobody will say anything.'

The Emperor's scratchy tenor floated down from the terrace above:

'Weep, weep, ye carven stones, ye hoary graven temples,
For scene more tragic ne'er appeared before ye!
Andromache, the faithful wife of noble Hector,
Brave Hector, hero son of royal Priam,

Bewails her infant thrown from off the Trojan walls,

Slaughtered to save the Greeks from later vengeance!'

Petronius shuddered delicately, but didn't even glance upwards. 'Be wary. Our lord and master seems to have little memory of the attack, and won't thank anyone who reminds him. Guilt, of course, but he'll never admit it, not even to himself. He's in a very queer temper. Natural enough, I suppose – if anything about him is natural . . . He keeps saying he can do anything he likes, no-one has the right to criticise someone who will be a god when he dies. That was Poppaea's mistake, it appears. Walk on eggs for a while, my precious plum.'

'Plums don't walk, let alone on eggs.' Sitting down, Pulcher tried to lighten the mood, but Petronius only huffed in exasperation and danced off.

Pulcher shrugged and beckoned Victoria to sit by him. 'Cheer up, Vicky. You know you couldn't have saved her. Nobody could. He could have attacked you if you'd gone in earlier, and if you'd defended yourself the Praetorians would have killed you – you know they're jealous, just waiting for an excuse.'

'I know, I know! But I heard him do it – and I can't help thinking, if I had only pushed in when the noise started, been there, been a witness . . . He might have stopped. I liked Poppaea.' She leaned against his shoulder for comfort. 'And the baby . . . I hate it when children die.'

'Sit up,' he told her. 'We're always being watched, remember. See that man in the corner, the thin rat-faced one? That's one of Tigellinus's men. He interviewed me the day after we arrived, ordered me to tell him if you ever spoke against Nero.' He grinned as she glared across at the man. 'Don't worry, I told him of course I would! He hasn't spoken to you? Lucky you! But we mustn't give him any arrows for his master to fire at us. Don't let him see us too close.'

Victoria for a moment let her head fall aside to nudge Pulcher's shoulder, as if accidentally, before she did as he said and sat upright again.

Above them, Nero's pacing had brought him to the balustrade. Glancing down, he saw Victoria's small gesture of affection. His chanting faltered as he frowned. He gestured irritably to a servant to retune his fabulous ivory lyre. Fondness, happiness, when he was suffering so? They had disrupted his mournful mood. How dare they!

What had Tigellinus said about them the other day? Disloyalty from his protective gladiatrix? Nonsense, of course, but . . .

XI

Ten days later, Victoria was not on the programme of the next set of games organised. 'Do you wish to attend, sire?' she asked at breakfast.

'No! I'm in mourning! My wife, my unborn child – how can I celebrate?'

'Dedicate the games in their honour, sire? The games started as a funeral offering to the dead, didn't they? It would be fitting, in a way, when the lady Poppaea loved the games so much.'

Nero considered for a moment, glowering at her. Abruptly he nodded. 'Yes . . . Yes, that's what I'll do. I'll go.' His face twitched. 'Better than hanging about the palace.'

However, as she walked by his chair in the procession an hour after noon, Victoria felt uneasy. Nero kept turning while he waved to the crowd, peeking aside at her and smirking. In his carrying chair behind, Petronius looked so serene and ignored her so completely that she knew he was worried too. What was the Emperor planning?

The Vestal Virgins were waiting, as usual, to scatter flowers before the Emperor before they took their own seats beside the royal box, directly above the Portus Triumphalis. Among a grove of fair-sized trees in carefully camouflaged pots in the arena black men dressed in brilliant loincloths, beads and turbans – the Roman notion of African tribal wear – were chasing giraffes with spears and chariots. At the trumpet fanfare they gave the beasts a brief rest while Nero regally acknowledged the cheers of the crowd and settled among his cushions.

As the hunt resumed, Nero beckoned. The editor of the games, waiting at the rear of the box, hurried forward to salute. 'Is everything ready?' the Emperor asked.

The editor's glance flickered to Victoria. 'Yes, sire. Everything is prepared.' He was stiff, not meeting her eyes.

She knew it! The fat imperial fart had something nasty planned. She should have killed him long ago.

Nero turned to her, sniggering. 'A surprise for you, Victrix! A chance to display your skill to the utmost, before the whole of Rome!'

Petronius's eyes and quick speech warned her not to argue. 'Oh, what good fortune, my amazing Amazon. On you go, and put on a superlative show!'

She bowed and followed the editor out in silence. As soon as they were out of sight, she grabbed his arm. 'Who? Who am I to fight?' But she knew. Oh, yes, she knew.

'Your fancy-man.' He grinned, gloating over the jumped-up virago getting slapped down – especially since he had bet on the man she had killed last time. 'The Emperor's not best pleased with you. He doesn't like rivals!'

She had been warned . . . They hadn't been careful enough . . .

Down through the dark tunnels under the seats, to a cell where her new armour was waiting for her – and Pulcher, already armoured, his scars gleaming pale in the yellow torchlight.

'No. No!'

Pulcher's eyes were dark and rueful, but resolute. 'Yes.'

'I won't!'

'You will.'

'I can't!'

'Yes, my love, you can. You must. We must.' He took Victoria firmly in his arms and held her while she shook with rage. 'Stop that, Vicky! Victrix! There's no time! Listen to me! Are you listening?'

Shuddering with the strain of trying to master herself, not howl in frustration, she nodded.

'Good. Control! You must control yourself, now if never! I've had an hour to think about this. Jealousy, spite, guilt, whatever, it doesn't matter, Nero wants me dead.'

'Or both of us,' she spat. She clenched her teeth to stop herself cursing him for being so honourable, for not loving her as she had wanted, for wasting time, when it all came to this in the end anyway.

'Or both of us,' he agreed, 'but I think not. No point in arguing, since there's no way we can find out. Come on, I'll help you dress.'

The familiar actions, the warmth of the padding, the weight of the armour, helped her contain her fury and fear. He tied and buckled as he spoke. 'There's only one chance for both of us to walk off alive. Thrill the Vestal Virgins till they vote for mercy. They're the guardians of Vesta's sacred flame that's the heart of Rome, even more important in some ways than the Emperor. If they meet a man on his way to execution, even for treason or murder, he's automatically freed. If they decide we should live, not even the Emperor can deny them. So we give the finest, fastest, most awesome fight this arena will ever see – and stop, leaving them gasping for more, so that they'll signal to let us live.'

He held her away from him and gazed into her eyes. 'Now, I don't want to die, and nor do you; but if it goes wrong and they call for death – quick and clean, remember.'

Better than a hideous death by torture. She nodded stiffly. 'You, too.'

He hugged her. 'Of course. My love, oh, my love . . .'

Yes, she'd do as he and Petronius said: put on a marvellous display. But she'd not rely on any Vestal Virgins. Nero was more likely to let her live, as the incarnation of his little dolly idol. At the end, she would make sure she was the one who had to beg for mercy.

She didn't see Pulcher's eyes dwelling on her determined, closed face. He knew her; he guessed what she planned. But he was sure that whatever happened today in the arena, in the Emperor's mind he was marked for death. Sooner or later he would meet a couple of soldiers come to arrest him for treason, or just a sharp knife on a dark night . . . But he could give the girl he loved a chance to live — if he died now, after showing her off as irreplaceable.

And pray to all the gods that she would control her temper.

A knocking on the door. 'Ready? The Emperor's waiting!'

Gently, they kissed. 'Helmet on, Victrix. Ready? Bags of swank!'

'We'll give your old granny something to remember!'

To show off everything they had, it was a long fight, the length of six normal pedestrian contests. Victoria and Pulcher worked together in perfect empathy, striking and parrying, spinning and dodging, fencing now with delicate jabs from behind their shields, now in great swooping swirls, in short, jagged flurries and in long-drawn-out walloping rallies. To the fight they had developed to please Petronius, they added extras they had been working on, and more that they invented spontaneously. Sparks flew from their swords as they fenced, clowned, somersaulted, wrestled. They moved, as they had done before, right round under the high barrier wall of the arena, but concentrated most of the action in front of

163

the royal box. The din of cheering could be heard a mile away.

Victoria was lost in the rapture of sacrifice; let her last fight be a great one . . .

The crowd got their fill of gore. Victoria sliced across Pulcher's chest, sheeting his belly with blood which trickled messily on down his legs. He slashed her thigh, she cut his neck. 'Neat!' Pulcher called – and stabbed her shield arm. The sand which soon coated their oil and sweat absorbed the blood, glowed crimson, matching their red clothes.

At one point Victoria dropped her shield. She wielded her sword with both hands for a whole desperate minute till she threw a handful of gravel at Pulcher's helmet; he backed off, pretending to be half blinded, which gave her the chance to run and recover her shield, brandishing it and crowing in glee.

Later, they both sent their swords flying, apparently from a too-hasty parry. That let them wrestle, instead of fencing, showing off their acrobatics for a couple of minutes, pretending to struggle, race, dodge, dive to reach the swords. When they broke apart, panting and seemingly exhausted, Pulcher squatted on his heels and flapped his hands to stop her. When she paused, he called to the arena slaves to bring them jugs of water. As the crowd laughed and cheered, they removed their helmets briefly to drink and pour water over their heads and aching hands.

The editor, not knowing them – or perhaps giving them an extra opportunity for drama – called on slaves with red-hot irons to drive them back to the fight, as if they were frightened novices or unwilling prisoners; they both acted insulted, seized the pokers and chased the slaves off and then the editor himself, throwing the hot irons after him to more laughter. Then they replaced their helmets, hefted their swords and the match continued.

Above them the crowd were almost as worn out, sobbing and moaning in excitement. Feverishly animated, Nero had flung aside his purple toga and his wreath. The white-robed Vestals, when either of the fighters could spare a glance, were leaning open-mouthed over their balustrade.

At last, Victoria's heart was bursting, her lungs heavy as leather, blood sheeting down her leg and arm, her hands swollen with wielding her sword and shield so long and hard. The half-healed wound in her hip would be a crippling agony, if she let herself pay attention to it. Reading her movements, understanding that she was done, Pulcher nodded to her.

She smiled faintly behind the grille of her helmet. Yes. Time to end it.

As exhausted as she was, Pulcher let her knock his shield from his hand. He jumped – lurched – forward to seize her sword hand in his left fist, and swung his sword. She lifted her shield, of course; she would pretend to be knocked off balance, let her sword slip loose into his hand, and fall, so that he would be standing above her with both swords, ready for her to kneel and ask for mercy – and surely, surely after this stupendous fight, it must be given?

But as his sword struck her shield, he released his hilt.

She watched the sword cartwheel and bounce across the gravel. 'No!' she whispered. 'No!'

Chest heaving, he turned to watch it with her. 'Don't waste it!' he wheezed, and sank to one knee, bowing his head, raising a hand towards the royal box.

All around, the crowds were yelling, signing for mercy.

Nero rose, beckoned for his gold wreath to be returned to him; raised a fist ready to give the signal; stood grinning, enjoying the tension, the power.

'What are the Vestals doing?' Pulcher panted.

Victoria peered up through the grille of her helmet. 'Looking at Nero.' The cheering was fading. 'No hands raised. Waiting to see what he wants.' She drew a deep, gasping breath. 'The stinking rat! Oh, no!'

Nero was signalling for death.

Pulcher's hand tightened on her knee. 'Quick and clean. I love you.'

Quick and clean. 'I love you too.' She stabbed down.

He crumpled against her feet.

In the sudden silence she tugged off her helmet and shrieked her war-cry. But not in triumph. Not this time.

Half drained of blood, head swimming with weakness, alone,

she forced herself to stay conscious, to stand upright above the body of the man she loved. At the cheering crowds, the fawning courtiers, the uncaring Vestals, the bloodthirsty Emperor, the whole world – from the roaring abyss of anguish and hatred they had blasted inside her heart, she screamed right into their enthusiastic, greedy, callous, non-comprehending faces.

She screamed defiance, and despair, and a vow of vengeance, on and on, sliding down, down the inside of a glittering whirlpool, into the peaceful dark at the foot.

XII

In dim lamplight, a boy was smiling, his eyes and teeth gleaming. 'A drink, miss?'

Where was she? Bed. Not the palace. A small, plain room, clean, white-washed, sweet-smelling, a tiny bronze hanging lamp, a high window with stars.

As the lad helped raise Victoria's shoulders, something clinked near her feet. She peered down. Her right ankle wore a ring of iron, linked by a chain to the side spar of the bed. She was fettered! She snarled in outrage.

'The mistress will come and speak to you in the morning. I'm so sorry, miss!' He was a slave, after all, not responsible – Victoria drank, and even made herself nod thanks before she sank back to the soft pillows. Pulcher, oh, Pulcher . . .

The water held a sedative. Her eyes closed.

Next day the lad brought a breakfast tray. Victoria made herself eat, porridge and eggs. She must recover her strength ready for vengeance. Oh, Pulcher . . .

Pulcher, smiling at her as he put on his helmet. Pulcher, her ideal, perfect match in that last glorious fight. Pulcher, kneeling before her. The jolt in her arm, and his weight slipping down her leg. Oh, gods, the loss! The empty, aching loss! 'I love you,' his last words. And she loved him . . .

Don't howl in desolation. Don't weep.

She could live through anything. She would live through this. Live long enough to avenge her love. Oh, Pulcher . . .

Don't weep. Never again. Control. That was what he had said. Control.

Caenis came in, dressed in dark green, with a stole of mourning black.

Victoria ignored her. This was a Roman.

Unspeaking, Caenis sat on the stool beside the bed, and drew a deep breath. 'The hurt in your hip is inflamed, but the other cuts are clean. You should recover soon, the physician says. From your wounds, at least.' Her face softened. 'My dear, I am so sorry.'

Aloof, Victoria lay silent, staring at the window. A bird was singing outside.

Caenis sat back, lips pursed. 'I can't blame you. But there are things you must understand, before you can leave.' She paused briefly, and her face tightened again. 'Frankly, if you refuse to accept them, you never will leave.'

That grabbed Victoria's attention. 'What do you mean?'

'Who would question that you died of your wounds? My people here know how dangerous you are to me, and they will keep it safely secret.'

'Dangerous? To you?'

'Yes. I don't mean that you would kill me yourself, though at present you want to slay Nero and every Roman, I can see it in your face. However, you could get me killed. I said if you needed help to come to me, but this . . . Nero has gone off east, sailing. But when he returns, or when he misses you and asks for you, you must either go to him or be dead. Five days, maybe, we can allow you, to reflect.'

The lady settled her black stole round her shoulders as if she was cold. 'If by then you are still set on instant revenge, I will kill you. You see, like you, I speak straight out.'

Victoria puffed, in reluctant respect. 'You do, don't you? Will you explain, lady?'

'You will listen. Good. I know how you feel – yes, I do. As a child, a born slave, I worked in the kitchen, always in trouble.' Victoria felt a sudden unexpected fellow-feeling. 'One day I fled from a beating, into a corridor I had never dared enter before. I ran right into the mistress, Antonia, almost knocked her down. She sent away the scullery-boy chasing me, gave me a fig, talked to me. Maybe she was merely bored, amused by a cheeky, desperate little brat. But she, the most noble lady in Rome, one of the imperial family, she took a liking to me, had me educated to become her secretary, her companion, even her friend. Without her favour, I'd have been a worn-out skivvy, and dead by now. When Gnaeus Mallio asked to buy me, to marry me, she gifted me my freedom, attended my wedding, and comforted me when he died only two years later. I mourned him, for he was kindly and gentle, but it was when my lady Antonia died that I – I was devastated. She had been so good to me . . .'

She sighed. 'Anyway, I know that you want to avenge your man's death. Appalling! You never-know with Nero. He switches from amazingly generous to disgustingly cruel, from astonishingly clever – occasionally – to incredibly foolish. He probably doesn't realise that he has offended you beyond forgiveness. But Tigellinus, who is never a fool, will have warned his men. If you attack Nero, you'll not get within ten paces of him before the Praetorians kill you.'

She braced her shoulders. 'Then Tigellinus will ask where you have been since the arena. If you had been carried to the slaves' infirmary in the palace, as you should have been, you would have died quietly in the night. Oh, yes. Tigellinus would never have risked letting you live to avenge your lover. So Petronius told the arena editor to send you to me instead. He stuck his neck out for you, far more than I'd ever have expected of him.' She chuckled wryly. 'You've made a fantastic impression on him! But he stuck mine out as well, Mercury take him! You do see it, don't you? If you go from here to kill Nero, I will be implicated. My slaves will be tortured to make them give evidence against me. I will be executed for treason. Probably so will Petronius, if he can't side-step it – and Tigellinus will do his best to see that he doesn't. However

171

much I like you, and I do, I will not – not! – risk my life, and all our lives.'

Caenis stood up. 'You must find a way to convince me that you will not bring us all into danger, before I can let you go. Rest, Victrix, recover. For five days. And consider what I've said.'

Victoria snorted in bitter amusement. 'Most carefully, lady!'

Though Caenis did not smile, she felt optimistic as she left.

Over the next two days Victoria thought hard. She must avenge Pulcher – oh, my love, Pulcher . . . Stop whingeing, concentrate! Control yourself! Avenge him, and Boudicca, and Britain. But yes, it was true; if she went straight out to kill Nero, even if she succeeded, which she reluctantly had to admit was unlikely, she would cause the deaths of many innocent people.

She realised; she had decided.

The next morning when Caenis came in Victoria was sitting up in bed. 'Lady, I agree. To seek instant vengeance would endanger you, and everyone who has helped me. You and Petronius. Your servants. Everyone in Glaevius's school. It wouldn't be fair.' She gritted her teeth. 'So I will swear to you, by Bouda, your Victoria, before whom I took my gladiator's oath, and before any other gods you wish, that I will not try to avenge Pulcher for a full year after I leave here. Will that satisfy you?'

Caenis actually clapped her hands in relief. 'Oh, yes! I am so glad! I'll send my steward Tiro out to buy a statuette of Victoria, and a sacrifice – what does your Bouda prefer?'

'A black she-goat, or even better, a hare.'

'Make your formal oath this afternoon, and we'll take off the chain. Forgive me if I hold you till then. I have the strictest instructions from Petronius—'

A skinny elderly man entered with a note. 'Forgive me for disturbing you, mistress, but the messenger says this is urgent.'

'Thank you, Tiro.' Caenis tutted as she read. 'Silly woman, always panicking! I'd better go. You drink your medicine, it will help you sleep, Victrix, and gather your strength. I'll return by noon.'

Victoria did as she was advised. She dozed, fighting against nightmares, and at last woke fully. It was early evening. No Caenis. Oh, well.

She stretched, carefully, and got up. Caenis had dressed her in a new blue tunic – a woman's one, but you couldn't have everything. She felt almost well again, though uneasy. Oh, Pulcher – No. Don't think about that. Think instead that her side hurt, but her leg and arm were almost painless.

There was no water left in the flask. She called, 'Lucius! Lucius, I'm thirsty.'

No-one answered.

She drew breath to call again, and stopped. And sniffed. Smoke.

A dull, distant roaring. Faint crashes and shouting. A red glow in the sky – not the sunset.

A fire. A big fire.

This was what had disturbed her dreams.

In Rome, fire was terrifying. The high, rickety tenements of the narrow streets, many of them thatched, built of thin plaster over wood, caught easily and burned fast and furiously. Even the bigger, better-built houses of the rich were packed close. There was a fire brigade, the vigiles, but if the wind was strong, flames could spread faster than you could run.

Victoria had a personal fear, too. She had been in a big fire before. Her scalp, her hands, her feet, all cringed in a spasm of dread. She couldn't breathe . . .

No! Control. She stamped hard on the flare of panic. 'Lucius! Anybody! Lucius!'

No answer. A big fire, close by; fire, and she was chained to the bed! 'Lucius!'

The boy scurried in. 'Oh, Miss Victrix—'

'It's coming this way?' He nodded. 'Where's the key to these fetters?'

He gulped. 'The mistress has it, and she's not back yet. Tiro is packing all the furniture in carts to get it away to safety.' The boy looked desperately scared.

Victoria couldn't just wait and hope Caenis turned up. 'Get me sandals, Lucius, and give me a hand.'

She made him help her raise the bed-head; then she smashed

it down as hard as she could. Lucius yelped in shock, but she insisted on doing it again and again, and eventually the joints cracked to let her kick the side spar out and slip off the ring of her fetters. With strips off the bedcover she tied the ring to her waist under her skirt and bandaged the chain to her leg, out of the way.

By the street door Tiro was telling a crowd of servants with bundles, 'No, I said, there's no more room! Now tie the covers down tight or we'll have half the stuff stolen. Oh, Praenax, what did Vitruvius say? No?' He cursed. 'What does the selfish git mean, he's got no space? His house could hold the Temple of Saturn! If he can't fit three carts into a corner of his garden . . .' He noticed Victoria. 'Victrix! Who let you loose? Lucius—'

'Were you going to leave me to roast?' As Tiro faltered, Victoria looked past him. Carts were standing outside, their mules tossing their heads, kicking and biting at the slaves holding them, and at the terrified mob jostling past them. Beyond, sparks were jetting high into the deep blue of the sky. She gritted her teeth; don't panic . . . 'What can I do to help?'

Tiro shrugged, deciding to concentrate on the flitting. 'Lead a cart, I suppose. Lucius, get her a scarf to keep the ash and sparks off her head – oh, Jupiter, there are the vigiles starting another fire-break.'

A gang of tired firemen in dirty leather tunics and helmets

forced their way through the streaming, screaming crowd, carrying poles, ropes and grappling hooks, and started to haul at overhanging roofs. 'Mind your heads!' their burly leader yelled. 'All this street's got to come down.' He pointed to the group of slaves at Caenis's door. 'Here, you four men, give us a hand! And you over there, too!' Soldiers arriving with him to stop looting grabbed one man who tried to run and kicked him thoroughly; the others angrily handed bundles and wailing children to frantic wives and joined the vigiles.

Tiro jerked a resigned head. 'Go on, boys, give the women your clubs, find us when you can.' He sighed, looking at the women, old men and youngsters he had left to control six terrified mules and save his mistress's valuable property. 'Antonia Caenis is a good mistress, so we'll do our best by her. Right? Let's get away before the vigiles grab the mules too! Keep together, hold their heads tight, keep your cudgels obvious. Everybody has two or three torches ready to light? Let's go!'

The mules plunged away from the frighteningly close flames and the crash of tiles smashing in the road behind them. No chance of them refusing to move, not today!

'How did the fire start?' Victoria shouted over the din.

'Over by the Circus Maximus, last night, nobody knows how. It's burned out half the mansions on the Palatine and the Carina, that's why nobody will take in the mistress's furniture, they're all full up with other people's stuff already. Now it's

176

heading here, so we're moving out. I wish I knew where the mistress was.'

Victoria glanced back. The fire was growing closer, moving faster than they were in the jammed streets. She must escape – but she'd not just flee . . . 'Look, a few days ago Nero gave me a house, the Villa Glauca. About three miles east, over the River Anio bridge. We can go there. Your lady has helped me; I'm glad to help her.'

Panting as he struggled to control his mules, Tiro considered, and nodded briskly. 'Right, thanks, miss.' Victoria smiled at the grudging respect. 'Lucius! You heard that? Nip back and tell the lads we left where we're heading for, tell the vigiles officer too in case the mistress comes back, and then catch us up; we'll go out the Esquiline Gate and up through the Necropolis.'

Lucius hesitated. Victoria didn't blame him. Though she felt like dropping everything and running, she made herself grin. 'Scared?' she asked.

'No!' Too loud, too defiant.

'So'm I.' She had once said the same to her cousin in Britain. Lucius looked startled, then relieved, and set off almost readily back up the road.

Tiro nodded approval. 'A good lad. He'll do.'

Victoria hoped she would, too. It was stupid to be so terrified, the fire was still a couple of streets away. But her belly was aching as badly as her hip, her hands and knees were trembling and her lungs felt heavy. She found herself actually leaning on the side of the cart for support as she limped along, buffeted and bumped by the mob of fugitives stampeding blindly under huge bundles.

When thieves attacked the carts the servants fought back valiantly. Victoria joined them, but found herself shockingly weak and was shoved back against the cart. She felt the old wound in her hip tear open again. Luckily, her scarf slipped off. 'Hoy, look out, it's that gladiatrix!' The robbers backed away, scared.

'The head comes in handy, eh?' She grinned, feeling better – action always relieved her tensions – padded the scarf and stuck it under the old bandage; that would have to hold the bleeding for now.

At last, the crowd squirted out through the Esquiline Gate in the old city walls. Narrow side roads let them squeeze north through the ancient Necropolis of Rome, where the crowds thinned, stopping to camp among the tombs and the old lime-pits where dead beggars and other rubbish were burned, or actually in the catacomb tunnels where some people buried their dead instead of cremating them tidily.

However, as they neared the crossroads outside the Viminal Gate they met a new flow of refugees also preferring to turn into the Necropolis rather than go out along the Via Valeria, which ran east across the mountains and on to the Adriatic Sea, the way Victoria and her group were heading. 'Three miles, you said?' Tiro asked wearily. 'Will the steward at your villa know you?'

Victoria shrugged. 'There's not many about with a head like mine! Hey, look, there's Lucius – and Caenis! They've come up the inside roads.'

Right in the middle of the gateway a high-laden ox-cart had lost a wheel and half its load, to the furious curses of the people struggling to get out. One was Lucius, holding a torch for Caenis to clamber out over the spilled bundles. Tiro let loose an astonishingly piercing bellow. 'Mistress! Antonia Caenis! We're over here!'

Lucius saw them waving and pointed them out. Surprisingly calm and elegant even amid the jostling mob, Caenis squeezed across the roadway towards them. 'Oh, you got out safely! Everybody? Good, I've been so worried! Tiro, did you get the jewels from the strongroom?'

Tiro nodded smugly. 'First thing packed, madam, all safe in the middle cart!'

'Well done!' She sighed in relief at the safety of her stock. 'I couldn't get back earlier. Placentia wasn't panicking as stupidly as I thought, the fire was right next door before we got her away, and her baby started arriving early, I just couldn't leave her. But I knew I could trust you – all of you.' Her servants beamed proudly.

At a trumpet blast from further along the road, demanding instant passage, Caenis skipped up to the pavement beside them. A troop of cavalry was cantering towards the gate. Any refugees who didn't dodge were trampled. The trumpet blared again, but at the wrecked cart the soldiers had to draw rein. Behind them a two-horse chariot driven by a man in a purple-and-gold tunic stopped not five paces away.

Victoria's heart clenched. Nero. The man who had made her kill Pulcher. He waved his whip at the collapsed cart. 'Clear that out of the way! Now!'

Her muscles were already tensing to leap when someone gripped her arm. Caenis. Victoria hesitated. She had sworn to wait – not formally, with a sacrifice, but she had said it – and could she betray the woman who had helped her?

As she swithered, Lucius shifted his torch, and Nero's eye was caught by Victoria's head. 'Victrix! Ah, wonderful! You see what happens when you're not with me! Rome is destroyed! I'm going to put out the fire, civil servants always need a guiding hand! Come along, jump up beside me here – my luck's come back!' He beckoned with his whip, clearly not suspecting any hostility.

The Praetorians around him moved forward protectively. Tigellinus had indeed warned them to watch her. Victoria scarcely noticed. Her legs were trembling as badly as her hands. Rome was destroyed? She patted Caenis's hand reassuringly and murmured, 'Don't worry!' before forcing herself forward. She didn't need to do anything, now, except avenge Pulcher, and she must wait a year for that.

But he was going towards the fire! She couldn't! She couldn't!

She called up, 'Caesar! My friend there, she looked after me, I was going with her to my villa, the one you gave me, but maybe the caretaker won't let her in without me. May I go with her, and return to you after?'

Absently, Nero shook his head. 'No, stay with me.' He beckoned a Praetorian. 'Attend to Victrix's friend – help her get settled. Get that confounded wagon off the road!' he screeched at the men labouring in the gateway. Saluting, the soldier tugged his mount out of the troop to speak to Caenis, as Victoria pointed her out. Caenis gave her a rather shaky smile.

As the wagon was finally shoved aside, the chariot jolted forward. Victoria scrambled to sit by Nero's feet. She had to go. Back to the fire . . .

But she would survive, and find a way to destroy him safely later. She waved farewell to Caenis. Rome was destroyed. Rome was destroyed. Rome was destroyed.

XIII

Rome was not destroyed.

More energetic and involved than Victoria had ever seen him, Nero did not just drive about spectating and ordering people about, but insisted on actually helping, joining in turn the gangs he visited. He used an axe surprisingly well; from his driving, his wrists and arms were stronger than anyone might expect, and he quickly got the knack of throwing the blade effectively. Though his presence worried the firemen, in case a tile fell on the imperial head, or a spark singed the imperial tunic, or an impious splinter pierced the imperial skin, it reinvigorated them and certainly quashed any arguments about houses being pulled down. The work went faster, and Nero's popularity soared.

Half the mansions on the Palatine had caught fire, including the Domus Transitoria. While the vigiles had concentrated there with their hooks and buckets and wet mats, losing only one wing of the palace, the blaze outside had spread beyond their control. However, eventually the wind changed, to blow the flames back over the already-burned ruins of a good part of the south of the city. Gradually, through the sweating, cursing, filthy night, the men got the fire under control.

All night Victoria did absolutely nothing. She was paralysed by panic.

Her mind seemed trapped in the past, in the horror of the fire in Londinium, where a blazing house had fallen round her while she crawled, crawled, crawled . . . The pain then, in her chest and hands and head, now returned to overwhelm her mind. She could again smell her hair crisping, feel her knees burning.

She scolded herself. She was safe. It was over, long gone. Just a memory. It was cowardly to cower away. Control. She should be ashamed of herself.

She was; but at every flicker of flame, every hot blast, she cringed further into the shadows, praying that no-one would see her, only just too proud to flee.

Two hours before dawn, Nero quite justifiably felt he had done enough. He had driven across Italy, and laboured all night. He was exhausted. And the fire was dying. Luckily, when he climbed back into his chariot to drive back to the Domus Transitoria he scarcely noticed Victoria still crouched there.

High-flown with pride in himself, ostentatiously wiping sweat and grime from his face, he announced to his cheering courtiers, 'I, your Emperor, have with my own hands saved Rome!' Recovering now that she was away from the fire, Victoria heard him describing his efforts, his efficiency, his instant grasp of the essentials of organisation, his heroic single-handed battle to drive back the blaze.

Petronius was ecstatic. 'I fear I have only now arrived, sire, for my horses and my driving are no match for yours. And I find you triumphant, glorious, the saviour of the city! Such administrative and practical expertise! Such courage and inspiration! Could Hercules do more? I beg you, give me the axe which you wielded, to cover with gold as a precious relic for the Temple of Jupiter!'

Nero basked in the admiration and applause.

'And tomorrow,' Petronius's voice was full of anticipation, 'tomorrow we can start planning the rebuilding!'

'Yes – yes! You always see the opportunities, Petronius!' Nero was delighted. 'I can start all over again. Well – half over again. If only the whole place had burned down! The whole city, even! Think of what I could do!'

He paused on the way out to talk to some of the other courtiers, including a magnificently decorated officer. Though Victoria had never actually spoken to him, she knew him well: Tigellinus, the Praetorian Prefect, who had sent a man to order Pulcher to spy on her.

Her heart was like lead. She had failed, failed – and could do nothing about it! Rome still stood. She had sworn not to avenge Pulcher, not for a year – maybe not sworn formally, but Bouda would desert those who broke vows, however casual, made in her name. And she was a coward, afraid of her memories, terrified of fire . . .

A thought came to her. She had not sworn not to avenge Britain.

In places the fire was still burning. If sparks flew far on the wind – with a bit of help . . . She could still destroy Rome.

When Nero finally fell into bed, he yawned mightily. 'Oh, what a day! And what a night! And tomorrow – yes. Yes. Oh, wonderful!' The mumble ended in a snore.

Acte smiled down at him, and at Victoria slumped on her pallet beside his bed. 'I'll bring you fresh clothes, Victrix. Sleep well.' She tiptoed out.

Sleep well? Later, maybe. Victoria forced herself to sit up. Her head was thick with weariness and her side was throbbing, but the wound had stopped bleeding, and she had no time to attend to it now.

Right. Nero would sleep till noon, at least. If she left now, heading for the baths, the guards would think nothing of it. But she could simply walk on into the burned part of the building and out past the guards there, in Caenis's crumpled, grubby blue gown like a kitchen slave on an errand. Tiro's scarf, bloodstains and all, would hide her tattoos. She could return to the baths after the guards had changed at dawn, really get clean, and be back before the Emperor woke. No-one would realise how long she had been away.

It worked perfectly. In under ten minutes Victoria was picking her way through the rubble down to the untouched

Forum, which was buzzing in the torchlight with refugees, politicians and sightseers.

This, the heart of the city, the great market halls, the lawyers' offices, the Senate House, the Temples of Vesta, of Julius Caesar, of Saturn which held the Treasury offices; this was what she must destroy.

She headed upwind, towards the stalls and workshops round the Campus Martius, the army's parade and exercise grounds, where hundreds more refugees were camping on the open areas. A fire here would be unsurprising.

As she walked, she argued with herself. Could she make herself do it? Did she dare to re-create the thing that terrified her?

She must. To atone for her cowardice, to salvage her honour, as well as to avenge the destruction of Britain, she must. She must.

Biting her lip to keep down panic she quietly lifted a burning stick from an untended campfire and walked off, nursing her little flame in trembling hands. She felt much worse than in combat, even though no-one in the bustle was watching her.

Now. She thrust her match through a fence outside a carpenter's workshop with piles of shavings in the corners, ideal tinder, which caught at once. She wanted to flee, but that would draw attention. Controlling her face, her jerking hands, her roiling stomach, she moved away.

Fifty paces further along, behind a ramshackle stable she lit the thatch of the house behind, and the hay inside a broken corner at the back, to let the mules get out – she didn't want to kill them!

Cries of alarm behind her. Everyone was looking that way. She walked on.

Three was the lucky number.

At a bigger yard, a builder's, she squeezed through the fence and bent to start her fire among dead grass in the middle, right in among the piled dry timbers.

'Hey, you!' An outraged bellow behind her. A big man was charging towards her, brandishing a two-handed saw that would rip her in half! She climbed frantically away up the stacked tree-trunks. 'Arson! A girl – blue dress – get her! Arson!'

Yelling, cursing her, the builder whirled the saw round his head and hurled it furiously. The unhandy missile bounced on the logs beside her, spanged up and lashed across her leg as she scrabbled over the fence, down into a lane of small shops and stalls.

Traders turned to peer towards the shouting, snatched to hold her. If they caught her they would tear her to pieces.

Victoria ran for her life, dodging automatically, knocking aside fists raised to grab her, sticks swinging to hit her. Curse these skirts! Her wounded side tore at her, but she had been well trained to ignore pain. A woman swiped her headcloth off, but she kept running. A corner, another, across a yard full of ramshackle tents, someone behind her tripped on a guy-rope and brought down all the first rank of her pursuers. A lane, two more corners, another yard, up and over the wall on the far side. Oh, Bouda give her strength!

Gradually she drew ahead of the roar of the chase. She jinked round four corners unnoticed and dropped to a panting, staggering walk. Safe!

Well, halfway safe. She still had to return to the palace.

Rather than going through the Forum she slipped through the half-burned market squares east of the Forum, trying to hide her limp. She found a torn cloth to cover her scalp; maybe it was so sooty that no-one had noticed it – make it so, Bouda!

Ahead of her, some men carrying torches were coming out of an abandoned house. Wasn't that furtive rat-faced one Tigellinus's man? He might know her. Glad she had seen them first, she hid behind a pillar till they turned away. Looting, maybe; she'd not put it past them.

Wavering up the Palatine Hill among the workers arriving for the day's labour, she paused to rest and look back. Her own fires were spreading across the Campus Martius, she could see the smoke. Several smokes, fairly widespread. She hadn't lit all those, had she? But they didn't matter; she had done it! Rome was destroyed this time, for certain!

A familiar voice startled her. 'Miss Victrix?' Lucius, grinning like a slice of melon.

'Sh!' She drew him hastily off to sit on a step beside the road. How lucky that he had seen her before he asked the palace servants for her, drew attention to her absence! What a sacrifice she owed Bouda for all her aid this morning! 'Is everything all right, Lucius? Did you get into my villa?'

'Fine, miss! The Praetorian didn't stand no nonsense, two minutes just and we were in, and the steward – he's a good man, looked after the place well – running about to make us welcome, hot water for a bath for the mistress in no time! So she sent me back to you with this.' Shamefacedly, he handed her the key to her fetters.

Victoria turned aside so that the passing people would not see her free herself, and discovered why the saw teeth hadn't bitten her; the chain tied down the side of her leg had acted as armour. Her dress was torn, but not her skin.

She handed the chain back to Lucius. 'Here. Antonia Caenis might want it again some day! No, don't worry, I don't blame her at all, or you! Tell her to use my house as her own. I'll come and see her as soon as I can. Thank you, and safe home, now!' She waved as he trotted off down the hill, and turned with a sigh to getting back into the Emperor's bedroom, past the Praetorians, without being noticed.

★   ★   ★

Bouda was still guarding her. After a good soak and scrub in the baths, Victoria got the bath slaves to rebandage her wounds and returned to Nero's bedroom door wrapped in a towel just as Acte was peeking in to see if he was awake.

The sweet girl smiled at Victoria. 'Fresh clothes as I promised, but not your sword, Victrix, I'm sorry, nobody knows where it is.'

Victoria smiled thanks. She'd find Needle later; she could scarcely have lifted it now in any case. It took all her strength to dress before collapsing on her pallet. By the time Nero eventually wakened she had managed a couple of hours' sleep, but it was restless, unrefreshing.

On hearing that the fires had restarted, Nero complained loudly, 'The vigiles couldn't put out the last embers without me, and let the fire recover? How inefficient! They should deal with it themselves!' However, he had enjoyed being a hero so much that he rattled about Rome in his chariot all afternoon, being cheered, but not today actually doing any work. In fact, Victoria got the impression that his orders were hindering, rather than helping. Maybe she was wrong; she felt dizzy and confused.

One of the stewards came looking for her that evening, while Nero was dressing for dinner. 'Victrix, spare me a few minutes, please. There's a small problem – if you come we can settle it directly.'

Sighing, she dragged herself to her feet and followed him

out and along the corridors to the entrance portico, favouring her aching hip. Oh, she wished Manny was here! 'What is it, Praxitides?'

'A nonsense, Victrix, but to stop any more rumours I thought we might just squash this one at once. There they are.'

Four men were standing in the hallway, one a senator in a toga, the others workmen in grubby tunics looking scared, but furiously determined. 'Tiberius Marcellinus, with three of his clients who wish to lay an accusation of fire-raising.'

Victoria's stomach knotted.

The senator looked righteously zealous; it was a patron's duty to support his clients, arson was a serious charge, and a big court case, daring to accuse one of the Emperor's slaves, could make him famous.

'Well, gentlemen?' Praxitides challenged them. 'Is this the person you say you saw?'

'That's the hag, sir! Know her anywheres!' one sobbed. 'She done it, burned me babbies!' Tears were rolling down his cheeks. 'Three on 'em, none on 'em five year old, lovely they was!'

Victoria's heart knotted too. Had she burned his family? Destroy Rome, yes, but babies . . . ?

The second brandished the bloodstained scarf. 'Yeah, that head, can't mistake it, I seen it, me wife snatched this off of it! But she dodged us near the Forum.'

The third was the big builder, as aggressively certain as the others. 'Aye, that's her! Hit her wi' me saw, that's what I done, me big saw, threw it at her, hit her leg, her right leg, that one there, an' see her limpin'? All ripped up she'll be. Let the hellcat show us her leg, the marks'll prove it!'

Such a flood of relief came over Victoria that she had to sway over to collapse on a marble bench at one side. 'You think I was out – when? Dawn today? Setting fires? Where? The Campus Martius? Well.' She sighed, in relief pretending to be resignation.

'First, I've been with the Emperor for the last two days. All the time. He'll confirm that.' All the accusers looked alarmed. Victoria hid a grin. 'Or Acte will, and she actually saw me here at dawn today.'

'I'll ask the lady to come here,' Praxitides suggested.

'Don't bother her for the moment. I think I can satisfy these gentlemen here and now that they've made a mistake.' Victoria tried to keep her mind clear. 'You wounded your arsonist? On the right leg? You're certain? Well, it wasn't me. I got two wounds in the arena some days ago.' She had to stop for a breath to steady herself. 'Anyone who was there will tell you. I only rose from my bed yesterday. I've been in no state to run about anywhere. I'll show you.'

She bent, wincing, to untie the cross-garters and roll up the loose legging on her left thigh. 'Here's one gash I got in the ring, and here –' she pulled up her sleeve and raised the edge of the bandage 'here's the other. You can see they're both healing, not made yesterday. I have another in my hip – wait till I pull up my shirt – See? That's why I'm limping, but this one's about fifteen days old.' It looked horribly red and swollen; one man winced at the sight of it. 'But those are the only hurts I have. Look.'

She rolled up her right trouser leg, to show clear skin. The chain had saved her from this accusation as well as from the teeth of the saw. Oh, how much she owed Caenis!

She smiled wearily at the tradesmen. 'Do you think I'm fit to be rampaging about lighting fires and fighting off crowds? Why should I, anyway? I'm truly sorry for your losses, but . . .'

At least half convinced, depressed, sensing the senator's annoyance that he might have made an influential palace enemy for nothing, they apologised. 'Sorry, miss, sorry, but when you've seen your children burn, an' your work an' your home . . . Not thinkin' straight, maybe. Sorry, miss!'

'No, I understand, it's all right,' she assured them, smiling to hide her guilt.

Swiftly, Praxitides sneered them out. 'Thank the gods for that!' he muttered, returning to Victoria. 'With these rumours going about, we can do without—'

Children burning? She felt sick. 'What rumours?'

He sniffed. 'That Nero had the fire restarted to clear enough ground to rebuild the city and palace the way he wanted. Not even Tigellinus would do that!'

Last night Nero had said that he wished he could rebuild

the whole city. And though he was so tired, he had been talking eagerly to Tigellinus. And the men with torches . . . Victoria's face must have shown her thoughts, for Praxitides suddenly clamped his mouth shut, and ushered her back to Nero's rooms without another word.

That evening, after dinner, the Emperor led his courtiers out onto a balcony that overlooked the fires. These had spread right across the city again, coating the slopes of Rome's hills in a bubbling froth of reds and oranges and black. The sky glowed red, sparks flying high above the burning, toppling houses.

He sighed in rapture. 'What a sublime spectacle! The burning of Troy, re-enacted here before me! Bring me my lyre! When the muse enflames a man's soul, who can resist her?'

'Not you, sire!' If Petronius's voice was a touch dry, Nero was too exalted to notice.

He posed dramatically with his ivory harp against the background of the agony of the city, and began to sing.

'Loud and fierce flames the inferno, the blaze of the terrible vengeance!
Loud roars the fierce Menelaus, seeking adulterous Helen!
Loud weep the women of Troy, but no tears can extinguish that furnace,
Loud cheer the warrior Greeks, slaying the terrified Trojans!
Loud shriek the children and babes lost in that furious furnace,

Vengeance of gods of Olympus, vengeance of ravening heroes!
Up sweep the sparks and the cinders, soaring on high to the
heavens!
Down drops the dark desolation, the breath of the demon
disaster!
Up fly the prayers with the flames, the smoke from the pyre of
the city!'

Victoria's head was aching as fiercely as her side. She had
been too sick to eat all day, and now felt quite faint. Even here
the breath of the fire was scorching, its voice a menacing
growl. She struggled to stay upright.

Beside her Petronius's face seemed to swell and shrink
like a reflection in a wavy mirror. His carefully controlled
expression of awed admiration seemed to change as he glanced
at her. She almost laughed; ridiculous! As if Petronius would
show alarm!

Nero's voice was fading and booming and fading. Vengeance
of the gods, women and children . . . Burning babies . . . She
hated it when children died. Had she . . . ? No, she couldn't
have, surely . . . Maybe she had . . Dreadful . . . She felt so
sick . . . Guilty . . . Fire . . . If only that unspeakable poetry
would fade completely . . .

Once again, as she had done just five days before, she fell
and fell and fell into that dark, welcoming whirlpool.

XIV

A month later Antonia Caenis herself carried out a beaker of well-watered Falernian wine to the terrace of the neat little villa overlooking the orchard and the river.

In a long chair Petronius Arbiter lounged in the shade of the pergola, half asleep. Victoria, lying on a padded couch beside him, set a finger to her lips. But at Caenis's footsteps he blinked and sat up, always alert for trouble.

Caenis set down her tray. 'Lie still, both of you. My customers have left.'

'A good sale, Caenis?' Victoria asked.

'Excellent! I've written to all my agents to buy all the semi-precious stones they can find: amber, agate, cornelian, fine marbles, lapis, mother-of-pearl – anything.'

Petronius, taking a cup of wine, snorted. 'This new dinky little bijou palacette is going to be coated with them. Nero has architects and interior designers buzzing round him as dead meat has flies.'

Caenis grimaced. 'Really, Petronius, your imagery can be sickening!'

He shrugged. 'Only natural, sweetheart! He's wallowing in an ecstasy of inspiration, planning the hugest, most ornate mansion in the world, with parks and a lake, right in the middle of the city. Well, where the city was. The Domus Aureus – the Gold House. He'd have it solid gold if he could.'

Victoria sipped thoughtfully. 'So. Rome survives.'

'It's actually spreading. It'll join onto Neapolitanum soon.' Petronius actually sounded depressed. He gulped some wine and lay back in his chair.

Caenis nodded agreement. 'Only about a third of the city was burned, and much of that was the Subura slums. No loss.'

'Except to the people who lived there.' And their families . . .

'Well, yes. But Nero is providing land for new houses outside the city – bigger houses, better built, healthier.'

'He has to, dear. He's not letting anyone in to see what they can rescue from the ashes – the amount of melted silver and gold his men are raking out of the ruins you would not believe!' Petronius didn't open his eyes.

'And he's blaming those new Jews for starting the fire?' Victoria asked.

Caenis waved a dismissive hand. 'Oh, nobody believes it, my dear. It's an unpleasant subject – you're sure you feel strong enough to talk about it?'

'I'll be training again tomorrow, lady, and ready for the arena in two months. No, don't look so doubtful, I will! So tell me.'

'Tigellinus's men were seen going about with torches. So Nero found he was extremely unpopular, and had to find somebody to blame.' Caenis twisted her shoulders in elegant distaste. 'He's executed two or three hundred of that Jewish sect. I didn't realise there were so many.'

Unmoving, Petronius smiled wryly. 'Like mice, dear. You never do realise how many there are, until there's a flood or something to drive them out. But they're terribly disappointing in the arena, won't fight at all, so our imperial master has to find new ways to kill them – crucifying them round the arena walls, or soaking them in tar and lighting them as torches for his parties. They don't burn well.' His voice was light; his expression grim. 'During a party he sent a messenger to the ones crucified in the arena, asking them could they die more quietly, please, as their moans were disturbing his guests. They did.'

Caenis made a face. 'Revolting, however dirty and unpleasant they are – not that I believe all the horrible rumours. Impiety, yes, which might anger our gods, but not all the rest – cannibalism, incest, treason—'

'Don't forget arson, my sweet!'

She nodded. 'They'd have faded away if nobody paid any attention to them, but now people are starting to say only a god could inspire people to die so bravely.'

She looked up as Tiro came out onto the terrace. 'Did I hear knocking?'

'Yes, mistress. Can you come, mistress?'

Rather surprised, Caenis rose and followed him into the house.

It was unusual for Tiro to ask for help in dealing with someone. Maybe it was Praetorians to arrest her, Victoria thought. But no; no-one had accused her of arson, not since that night. She had Nero's permission to be here, and good wishes for a speedy recovery. Not that he was missing her – or that she was in any hurry to return to him.

What should she do, though? Rome still stood. Nero still lived.

First, get well and fit. She couldn't do anything till then. And cure herself of this ridiculous, degrading fear of fire!

Caenis returned, beaming – clearly not Praetorians. 'Visitors for you, Victrix, not for me. Friends from Pompeii!'

Victoria gasped in delight at the two bright figures who marched out to grip her hands and grin at her. 'Divina! Africa! How wonderful to see you! Are you fighting in the arena here?'

Languidly Petronius rose, waving a casual hand as the two visitors bowed to him. 'We'll leave you to chat, my pet. Old friends are always better savoured alone. In any case, I must return to see what delights his Imperial Majesty has dreamed up in my absence.' He and Caenis returned to the house. He would naturally avoid having to do with gladiatrixes unnecessarily; it had been polite of him to make an excuse.

Victoria was eager to hear the news – and reluctant to speak of her own. 'How is everybody? Have you – have you heard about Pulcher?'

Her friends' mouths twisted. 'Yes, we hear,' Divina said. 'Bad luck. For you an' him.'

'We were all angry. He was a good man.' Africa nodded soberly. 'But Glaevius –' She stopped.

'What's wrong with him?'

'He dead,' Divina said sadly. 'When he hear, he curse, curse, his face go purple, you remember? An' he fall. Dead.'

'Rhadamanthus judge his spirit kindly!' Victoria whispered. 'What's happened to the school?'

'His nephew inherit.' Divina's tone was disgusted

'And he's ruining the place!' Africa snarled.

'Useless as fart in thunderstorm!'

'He wanted to put slave collars on everybody, even the volunteers!'

'Idle sponge!'

'He sacked half the trainers to save money.'

'Try tell us we can't go out when we want!' Divina spat, copiously.

'So,' Africa finally took over the story, 'since Divina's contract was up, she and I have decided to start up a school on our own, of gladiatrixes –'

'The Amazons!' Divina announced, posing proudly, fists high.

'I bought myself out, and Divina bought out four of the rest, cheap because he disapproves of women fighting and doesn't know our worth. So we've come to see if you'll join us!' They sat back and beamed at her.

'Wow!' Victoria was breathless. 'I'd love to – but how? I'm contracted for five years.'

They looked dumbfounded. 'You not know?' Divina demanded.

'Know what?'

'Pulcher buy you out.'

Africa nodded confirmation. 'Before you came to Rome, he came to see Glaevius and bought you free. A hefty price, too.'

'*What*? Why didn't he say?' Victoria was flabbergasted. 'How could he afford it? Why didn't he tell me?'

Rejoining them, Caenis tutted at the visitors. 'Please don't upset my patient! She almost died, from a wound in her side that went bad, and she's not fully recovered yet. Take some wine, do, and tell me what's the matter.' As they explained, her face grew serious. 'Oh, what a fine, deep-thinking man your Pulcher was, Victrix! How could he tell you, without seeming to be trying to buy your love? Or maybe upsetting your fighting—'

'Good thought!' Divina approved.

Slowly, Victoria nodded. 'But – when I think of the time we wasted . . .'

Divina looked sympathetic. 'He not—'

'No, he didn't.' Victoria blushed. Stupid! Control . . .

'How you stay so shy, eh?' Divina snorted with astonished laughter. 'Pulcher not want you get tangle.' Her face changed. 'But you tangle anyway. With Emperor.' She spat again.

There was no safe comment to that.

After a moment, Africa reached into a purse hanging from her belt. 'Publius Natronis — he's our lawyer in Pompeii — he asked us to bring you this letter.'

Still in a whirl, Victoria broke the seal and opened the stiff parchment. 'Look — my certificate of freedom is inside!' But as she read the lawyer's letter, her jaw dropped.

'Come on, then, tell us!' Africa urged her.

'It's — it's about Pulcher's will. He's left everything he owned to me. And he inherited from his adoptive father — he was rich! Houses and land and money — nearly half a million sesterces — a fortune! I could even buy the palaestra myself!'

Divina and Africa gazed at each other with dawning glee, and plunged into eager argument about the best way to go about it.

Victoria lay back, dazed. After a few minutes, Caenis intervened quietly. 'Enough for now, Divina, Africa. Let poor Victrix have time to take in all this news. You have lodgings in Rome? Good. Then come back tomorrow, come and dine with us, if that suits you, Victrix? It is your house, after all.'

'Oh, yes, yes of course! Let me think about it, please! It's all too much, all at once. Let's discuss it tomorrow.'

Victoria stirred herself to sit up and wave as they left, still arguing. Then she collapsed with a puff of weariness. If she had been alone, she would have asked them to stay with her, but she understood why Caenis had sent them off. As an ex-slave who had to take care of her reputation, Caenis was risking enough malicious gossip by sharing Victoria's house even in an emergency, without adding another pair of low-lives to the household. Her invitation to dinner was an amazingly courteous, almost revolutionary gesture.

'Thank you for sending them away! I love them, but . . .' Victoria sighed. 'I am really grateful to you for everything. You've been so good to me, running my house, nursing me like a baby while I was raving — you've saved my life so often—'

'Nonsense, Tiro and the servants do all the housework, and I could scarcely leave you to die when I was your lodger!' The corners of Caenis's eyes crinkled pleasantly as she smiled. 'This house suits me very well for now, it's comfortable and very pleasantly situated away from the worst of the refugees, but near enough Rome for my customers to reach me and enjoy an agreeable outing at the same time. Nobody wants to buy jewellery after the fire, but with this new palace, my sales are increasing, if anything. If you're grateful to me, well, I'm grateful to you. When both sides are happy, it's good business.'

She refilled Victoria's cup. 'But they really couldn't stay here. You need some time to consider what you want to do. Which may not be the same as what they want, though they are your friends.'

Victoria sipped her watered wine. It was a while since she had thought about what she herself, wanted. As a slave, and bound by a geas, she had had little freedom of choice. But now . . .

She could retire from the arena. Did she want to? No; being a gladiatrix was still her life; there was nothing she would rather do. Not yet, anyway.

Buy the palaestra? No; it would remind her too strongly of Pulcher. Besides, it was the fighting that she enjoyed; Glaevius had spent most of his time organising food and armour, replacements and fights. Not for her!

So what would she do?

They sat in silence for a while, relaxing quietly, listening to the river, the birds, the laughter of Caenis's servants in the kitchen.

A thought gradually developed in Victoria's mind. She had realised long ago that fighting in the arena was no good as a way of destroying Rome. She should be aiming at the nobs, Nero himself and his toadies. Burning the city had only hurt ordinary people. Children . . .

If she killed Nero, the next man would probably be just as bad.

The finest way to avenge Boudicca and Britain and Pulcher – oh, Pulcher! No! Control! Don't weep! The best thing she could do for them, and for the whole of the world, when she thought about it, and the very worst thing for Nero and his arrogant courtiers, would be not just to kill him when the year was over, but to replace him. With a good Emperor.

Someone new, not from the decadent, vicious imperial family.

Someone trained for the job, experienced in command, not just inheriting it, or murdering his way into it.

Someone efficient, intelligent, honest, hard-working, tough, brave, reliable, determined, sensible, decent.

Someone with good sons to support and follow him.

Someone popular among the people with actual physical power – and that meant the army, not greedy, corrupt officials.

Someone who could take the whole rotten Empire and its trashy government, shake out the rubbish, clean it up and lay it out straight and tidy.

And she knew who.

But how? And could one girl alone ever manage it?

Don't despair! She had felt this dismay when Boudicca had first set the sacred task on her, and alone had done a fair bit towards it. Finishing it could be no harder.

Oh, Pulcher . . . No. Control.

A rich, famous gladiatrix might find a way.

But not alone. She needed help.

Divina and Africa would support her as far as they could, in their own way.

But she needed someone of a different class, who could advise her about how Roman society worked, how the nobs thought, how to affect them best.

Petronius? No; he was too closely tied to Nero. Like Tigellinus, the Emperor's fall would bring him down too. He'd never agree to help. She was sorry that he'd probably be involved, damaged, by what she planned – but he had done very well out of the Emperor, was at least partly responsible for the way Nero behaved, and had brought her and Pulcher to Rome – Oh, Pulcher! . . . Stop that! Control; she must be ruthless. Petronius was clever enough to see trouble coming, and wangle himself out of it – and she'd warn him if she could, as he had warned her. But if he was hurt, he was hurt. Pity, but too bad.

No; she needed someone who would gain from what she hoped to do. Someone generally well-liked and trusted, who went everywhere and knew everyone, both nobles and workmen. Someone discreet who could find out and pass information to her, and talk to the right people . . .

Antonia Caenis.

If she was willing to.

It was a hugely terrifying, madly dangerous project. If they were even suspected . . . Traitors were hurled off the Tarpeian

Rock, a cliff on the highest hill in Rome, to die on the jagged rocks below.

And Caenis might not want to load her man with such a hugely terrifying, madly dangerous job.

But if they succeeded, he'd be able to keep her in the style she was used to . . .

'Caenis, if Nero died, who would be the next Emperor?' Victoria asked casually. Caenis looked alarmed. Victoria grinned faintly. 'Don't worry! A year I said, a year I'll wait. By then you'll have been in your own house for months. But just for interest – who?'

Caenis's lips pursed. 'Nero is still young, and may have children. If he doesn't – I don't know. There are so few of the imperial family left, just a few far-out cousins. If there's no clear heir, the senators should decide, or perhaps return to a republic. But these days they're as decisive as headless hens. All the strong-minded ones have been killed off, they couldn't decide what sandals to put on without a slave to help them. Julius Caesar, and Marius and Sulla – they were dictators before Caesar – they gained power with their soldiers, marching on Rome. It was the Praetorians who put Claudius on the throne, not the senate. So I suppose they'd do it again. Pick their favourite – or whoever offers them most extra pay.'

'Hmm. Just the Praetorians? What about the rest of the army? There are – what? – thirty legions, spread all over the world? Don't they have a say?'

Caenis laughed. 'They're not here in Rome.'

That didn't mean their opinion had no weight, though. Not if they moved on Rome as Caesar's men had done – or even if the Praetorians, and the senate, and everybody thought they might.

Well.

Never try, never win.

Caenis was studying her quizzically, clearly wondering just what was in her mind.

Perhaps she should approach this sideways, delicately – but she didn't know how. Straightforward. Then at least you knew where you were – even if it was deep in trouble.

Victoria sat up and drew a deep breath. 'Antonia Caenis, there is a matter of importance that I should like to discuss with you. About your friend, Vespasian . . .'

Glossary

Roman/Latin words are shown [L]

Celtic words are marked [C]

aedile [L]   Roman official who ran a city's police, firemen, markets

Aesculapius [L]   Roman god of healing

Arethusa [L]   fountain where the Muses, the spirits of all the arts, lived

as [L]   copper coin (4 asses = 1 sesterce; a loaf cost 1 as)

bard   druid specialising in music; singer, harpist

Bouda [C]   Celtic goddess of victory

Campus Martius [L]   old army exercise grounds

Carina [L]   area of Rome

centurion [L]   the Roman army equivalent to a staff-sergeant; a legion under-officer in charge of a century

Circus Maximus [L]   racetrack

client	supporter of an important man, in return for money, protection, favours
consuls [L]	two officials elected every year, to the highest elected position in Rome
Dionysus [L]	Greek god of wine, wildness
Domus Aurea [L]	Nero's new palace in Rome
Domus Transitoria [L]	Nero's first palace in Rome
druid [C]	Celtic professional priest, doctor, teacher, judge, etc.
editor [L]	manager of games in the arena
equestrian [L]	Roman citizen of rank just below the patricians; knight
Forum Romanum [L]	the oldest public square in Rome, where the Senate House, main city temples and offices were situated.
freedman	person who used to be a slave
fresco	wall painting, done on wet plaster
geas [C]	Celtic commandment from the gods; breaking it meant death
gladiator [L]	professional fighter in arena; usually a slave, despised by everyone including non-fighting slaves. However, champion gladiators

	were celebrities, like modern-day footballers.
gladiatrix [L]	female gladiator; even more despised than a gladiator
governor [L]	chief Roman official of a province, e.g. Britain.
Hermes Trismegistus	Greek god who was the guide of the dead (the Roman equivalent was Mercury)
Iceni [C]	Roman name for British tribe
Isis [L]	chief Egyptian goddess
Jupiter [L]	King of the Roman gods
lanista [L]	head of gladiators' school
legate [L]	Roman officer in command of a legion
legion [L]	Roman regiment of about 5,500 men
Londinium [L]	London
lyre	harp
Mars [L]	Roman god of war
Massilia [L]	Marseilles, in France
Mercury [L]	Roman god who led souls of the dead down to the underworld
Mithras	Middle Eastern god of light; became popular among soldiers

Necropolis [L]	literally means 'city of the dead' – a cemetery; by law, outside city walls
nymph [L]	Roman nature spirit
Olympus	mountain home of the Roman and Greek gods
palaestra [L]	training yard of a gladiatorial school
Palatine [L]	hill in Rome, with imperial palaces and mansions
patrician [L]	Roman of top class, descended from one of the founding families of Rome
patron	important man who has clients to support him, to vote as he wants, etc.
praetor [L]	Roman magistrate and judge in law courts
Praetorian Guard [L]	legion of soldiers in Rome who were the personal guards of the Emperor
prefect [L]	Roman commander
procurator [L]	Roman official in provinces, in charge of money, taxes, coinage, trade deals
provocator [L]	gladiator with big shield, small breastplate

quaestor [L]	Roman magistrate in charge of taxes and money supply etc.
retiarius [L]	gladiator with net and trident, no helmet, armoured left arm
Rhadamanthus [L]	Roman god who was the judge of dead souls
Saturn [L]	Roman god of time, father of Jupiter
Scythia [L]	area north and east of the Black Sea; approximately modern-day Chechnya
secutor [L]	heavy-armed gladiator
senator [L]	member of Roman Senate, or Parliament
sesterce [L]	silver coin
Subura [L]	slum area of Rome
Thracian	light-armed gladiator
titan	giant
torc [C]	neck ornament, open C-ring of twisted gold or silver wires
tribune [L]	young officer assisting legate, general or other official
trireme [L]	galley ship with three banks of oars
Vesta [L]	Roman goddess of the hearth and home; the heart of Rome
Vestal Virgins [L]	six priestesses of Vesta

Via [L]	road, e.g. Via Appia
Victoria [L]	Roman goddess of victory
vigiles [L]	firemen
Yahweh	Jehovah, Jewish name of God.